ASHES BEFORE THE STORM

SERIES PREQUEL

ASHWING ASCENSION ADVENTURES

CANDICE BUNDY

PIPER FOX

LUSIOS PUBLISHING

CONTENTS

CHAPTER 1
SHADOWS AT SUNSET
ADARA

AGAINST THE NEWLY RISEN MOON, THE CRIMSON Veil Coven's border fortress rose like a fever dream of twisted spires and writhing shadows. The last traces of sunset stained the western sky blood-red, but darkness hadn't completely claimed the fortress grounds. Ancient magelights lined the fortress walls, their cold radiance casting stark shadows across weathered stone. Gothic drama queens, the lot of them. Everything I'd heard about vampire architecture proved true.

I stood before its gates. The fortress loomed above me, all sharp angles and dark grandeur that screamed *we're powerful and don't you forget it.* Though really, would it kill them to add a splash of color? Maybe some cheerful window boxes with petunias? I could just imagine the fortress's real estate listing: Charming evil lair, perfect for the discerning immortal. Features include excellent shadowy corners for brooding, gratuitously pointy spires, and absolutely zero natural light. All-black dress code is strictly enforced.

My boots crunched on gravel that shouldn't have been so... gray. A stray breeze lifted my fiery curls, and between the harsh magelights and ghostly moonlight, they rippled like flames in a draft. I absently tucked them back, as if by taming their wild energy I could control the outcome of my mission of the month.

The corruption hit me then. A bitter, metallic tang coated my tongue, the air pressing against my skin with an oily weight that made my stomach turn. Where evening birdsong should have filled the air, an unnatural silence reigned. Near the fortress walls, vegetation had withered into shapes that hurt my eyes, branches twisted into impossible angles that mocked nature itself.

Heat stirred beneath my skin, my phoenix fire responding instinctively. Well, that explained the urgent summons. Someone had been playing with powers they shouldn't. Likely those containment crystals the coven had "borrowed" from the Mage's Council last month. And now they needed the Elemental Phoenix to contain the fallout. Just another day shepherding immortals away from their own destruction.

Delightful.

A sickly purple-green glow flickered at the edge of my vision like a bruise in the sky, sending a wave of nausea through me when I tried to focus on it. The glow vanished when I looked directly at it, but its presence remained. An otherworldly force that bent reality itself. Shadows stretched impossibly long. Colors bled at the edges of my vision. Whatever was out there, it didn't belong in this realm. Or any realm, for that matter.

"Lady Phoenix." A voice cut through my observations,

the kind of voice that made you lean in before you remembered you shouldn't. The sound sent an unwelcome shiver down my spine, my flame-script flickering traitorously in response. I told myself it was just the corruption in the air. "We've been eagerly awaiting your arrival."

I turned to find a vampire noble descending the fortress steps, each movement deliberate enough to draw the eye despite my best intentions. The magelights caught the planes of his face. Sharp cheekbones, pale gray eyes flecked with red, a sign of recent feeding or perhaps agitation. The moonlight silvered everything it touched. His perfectly tailored black coat and the signet ring on his right hand marked him as high ranking, yet he'd come to greet me himself rather than sending a servant. I wondered if looking devastatingly handsome while radiating mysterious danger was a job requirement or just a happy coincidence. Because what I really needed right now was to catalog how unfairly attractive my potential problems were.

His gaze dropped to the permanent markings on my forearms: intricate burn patterns that resembled flame-script but remained static, unlike the living patterns that shimmered across my skin. I resisted the urge to cover them. The scars from that fae crystal explosion were a reminder that even my own power could mark me permanently.

But the tension in his shoulders didn't match the polished demeanor. That's what snagged my attention. Here was someone whose careful control was already fraying, unusual for a vampire of his rank... and annoyingly intriguing. My flame-script pulsed in what I chose to interpret as warning rather than interest.

"Have you now?" I arched an eyebrow. Sparks of irritation danced beneath my skin, my flame-script shimmering faintly in response. "It's Adara Ashwing, and have you been eagerly awaiting me, or eagerly awaiting what I can do for you?"

His lips curved into a charming smile that didn't quite reach his eyes as he studied me with unsettling intensity. The magelight glinted off the edge of his fangs, a subtle reminder of what he was.

"I'm Lord Evander Nightshade," he said. "I've been assigned to assist you during your stay."

"Assigned to assist me? Or assigned to watch me?" The air around us warmed slightly as my annoyance grew.

"Can't it be both?" His smile shifted, something almost genuine flickering through. "The coven takes its hospitality very seriously."

I snorted. "I'm sure it does. Almost as seriously as it takes its collection of artifacts that definitely belong to it and weren't at all acquired through questionable means?"

Evander didn't even have the grace to look embarrassed. "You've heard about that?"

"Word gets around when you steal from the Mage's Council. Especially when it's their prized collection of containment crystals." I started up the steps, forcing him to either move or be walked through. He chose to fall in beside me, matching my pace with unsettling precision, close enough that I caught something cold and faintly dusty beneath the expected iron tang of a recent feeding. I pointedly ignored how my skin prickled at his proximity. The scars on my legs tingled, a phantom reminder of my last encounter with Mage's Council containment magic. Their "controlled" spells could be just as dangerous as what they were trying to contain. Irony at its finest.

"I was curious what was worth risking their wrath. Must be something pretty special to have the Crimson Veil breaking its precious protocols."

"That's..." He hesitated, his polished facade cracking just enough to show actual concern. "That's something best discussed inside. Away from prying eyes."

I glanced around at the very obvious lack of anyone else in sight. The withered vegetation wasn't going to be spreading gossip anytime soon. But fine, if he wanted to play cloak-and-dagger games, I'd play along. *For now,* I added silently, just to make myself feel better about capitulating.

"Lead the way then, Lord Nightshade." I gestured to the towering doors ahead, my tone just shy of mocking. "Show me what was worth starting a magical arms race for."

He winced slightly. "It's not quite like that."

"No?" I watched him carefully, noting how his shoulders tensed at my question. "Then what is it like?"

Instead of answering, he pulled open one of the massive doors, his arm brushing mine as he stepped past. The entrance hall beyond was lit with floating orbs of crimson light that pulsed like heartbeats, casting everything in shades of blood and shadow. The orbs' light drained warmth from the air, leaving behind a bone-deep chill even my phoenix nature couldn't quite shake. I wasn't sure if it was the vampiric magic or Evander's proximity making the cold sharper.

But it wasn't the dramatic lighting that made me pause. It was the wrongness in the air. The same feeling I'd noticed outside, but stronger. The taste of iron had intensified to a caustic burn, and tendrils of corruption writhed against my skin like hungry serpents, probing for weakness. Because of course they were. Why would anything in a vampire fortress be simple?

"Come," Evander said. "The council awaits. And, Lady Ashwing?" His gaze found mine, and he stepped closer than was strictly necessary. My flame-script pulsed in warning. Or was it anticipation? Either way, the air between us charged with an awareness that had nothing to do with professional courtesy. "Try to keep an open mind about what you're about to see."

Oh, that was never a good sign. In my experience, "keep an open mind" usually translated to "please don't immolate us when you see what we've done."

I sighed, my breath visible in the unnaturally cold air. Between the wrongness pervading the fortress, the political games I'd inevitably have to play, and the inexplicable pull of a vampire who was definitely more dangerous than he appeared, this was going to be one of those jobs.

"Keep it together, Ashwing," I muttered under my breath. "Just another vampire fortress full of stolen artifacts and mysterious corruption. Totally routine."

CHAPTER 2

A DANCE WITH DARKNESS

ADARA

THE COUNCIL CHAMBERS LAY AT THE HEART OF THE fortress. With each step deeper into vampire territory, my phoenix fire stirred uneasily. Pulsing crimson orbs were everywhere, their blood-red light catching on the towering tapestries that lined our path. Centuries of vampire victories woven in threads of gold and crimson. The artistry was impressive, if you could overlook the obvious propaganda. Subtle, these were not. I wondered if they had a dedicated tapestry weaver on staff. *Yes, Lord Bloodfang, I can absolutely add more dramatic billowing cloaks to that battle scene. And perhaps another lightning bolt in the background? We want to make sure everyone knows how terrifying you are.*

I'd faced vampire nobles before in other lives. Their politics always ended in blood and betrayal. Yet Evander's presence beside me felt different from those ancient memories, his careful proximity more steadying than threatening.

The wrongness grew stronger here, that caustic iron

taste from outside now sharp enough to make my teeth ache and my throat constrict. The corruption twisted through the air in visible ribbons of sickly purple-green hues, like poison seeping through veins.

My boot heels clicked against marble floors, each step jarring in halls designed for silent predators. Beside me, Evander moved with that infuriating vampire silence, though I caught him watching me from the corner of his eye. That cold, faintly dusty scent still clung to him, more noticeable now in the enclosed space.

"The council has gathered in the Grand Chamber," he said, voice pitched low enough to brush against my skin.

I noted the conspicuous absence of any other vampires in the hall. "Empty, isn't it?"

"The council requested privacy," he said, his tone careful in a way that caught my attention. "Not everyone agrees with their... methods."

"Speaking from experience?" I asked, catching the edge in his voice. There was a story there, something that had made his shoulders tense. The shadows around him moved with a mind of their own. They curled around his feet, casting them into darkness.

His eyes met mine. I wanted to pull those secrets from him one careful question at a time.

"Let's just say I understand the cost of defying tradition."

The passage twisted deeper into the fortress's heart, its walls rippling rainbow-sheen obsidian where the corruption had eaten into the stone. Ancient preservation spells fought against the decay. They created patches where time itself stuttered. Moss grew backward, crumbling to dust before blooming again in endless cycles. Just when I thought vampire interior design couldn't get more dramatic, they'd managed to add reality-bending horror to their repertoire. I supposed normal hallways were simply too mundane for immortal beings. Why have straight walls when you could have ones that twisted your mind into knots? Though I had to admit, it made for one hell of a conversation starter at parties.

Evander's arm brushed mine. Heat flared where we touched, sharp and undeniable. The miasma surged stronger, each breath burning like acid in my lungs. My fire stirred restlessly beneath my skin. It spread through my veins like molten gold, trying to burn away the taint. The iridescent energy writhed against my defenses, probing for weaknesses just as it had in the entrance hall. Whatever corruption tainted this place, it was stronger the deeper we ventured into the fortress.

"The council chambers are just ahead," Evander said. He paused before a set of doors that seemed to absorb light rather than reflect it. Their surface shifted like oil on water, the carvings moving through an endless cycle of war and peace, victory and defeat. Each loop showed subtle changes, as if the history they portrayed was being constantly rewritten. His hand caught my elbow, the touch fleeting but deliberate. "A word of advice?"

I turned to face him, suddenly aware of how close we stood in the narrow space. "Let me guess. Watch my tongue, mind my manners, and try not to set anyone on fire?"

His lips twitched, gray eyes warming. Appreciation? Or was I reading too much into a vampire's expression?

"Actually, I was going to suggest you pay attention to what they don't say as much as what they do."

The sincerity in his voice caught me off guard. My fingers twitched, phoenix fire instinctively rising to my skin, but for the first time since entering vampire territory, the defensive response felt wrong. Unnecessary. I let the flames die back, watching his eyes track the movement with neither fear nor hostility. Just that same steady watchfulness that made my pulse jump for entirely different reasons.

The doors swung open silently. Because of course they did. They revealed a circular chamber that would have made any theatrical director weep with joy. Tiered seating rose in concentric rings like some sort of undead amphitheater, occupied by vampire nobles who managed to look bored while still being absolutely menacing. They'd really mastered that *I could kill you but I'm too aristocratic to care* expression. I wondered if they practiced it in mirrors. Though wait, that wouldn't work, would it?

The same purple-green energy that tainted the corridors writhed through the air here. The surfaces shifted between marble and a scaled texture when viewed directly. A red-haired vampire in the second tier leaned forward, hunger flickering in his eyes as he studied me. Beside him, a woman with frost-white skin twisted her rings nervously, the gems catching the red light with each turn.

In the chamber's center, a massive table of living crystal pulsed with captured starlight, its surface scarred by the corruption's touch. Where the purple-green energy met the celestial light, reality fractured into prismatic shards that hurt to look at. Stolen artifacts were scattered across its surface.

"The phoenix graces us with her presence," a voice announced from the highest tier. A female vampire with silver-streaked dark hair rose, her crimson robes marking her as head of the council. Power emanated from her in waves that made the air feel charged. Unlike the others, her eyes held no hunger or fear. Only calculation. I recognized that look from the Blood Wars of the third dynasty. It was the same expression the vampire queen had worn before ordering the massacre of an entire bear-shifter clan.

"I am Councilor Morana. Thank you for answering our summons."

I straightened under the council's collective gaze, letting my fire simmer just beneath my skin. Let them posture with their power plays and dramatic architecture. We both knew who held the real advantage here. Phoenix fire was anathema to their kind; my inferno could reduce their precious council chamber to ash, along with everyone in it. These vampires might be ancient and deadly, but they were also desperate. Desperate enough to risk bringing living fire into their sanctum. Whatever lurked beneath their fortress, whatever caused that malignant wrongness in the air, it had them terrified enough to seek help from their natural enemy. Now that was interesting.

Focus, Ashwing, I reminded myself. *Cataloging vampire desperation, not... whatever this is.*

"Councilor." I nodded, then gestured to the table. "I'm Adara Ashwing, and I suppose my curiosity got the better of me. I must say, this is quite the collection you've acquired. The Mage's Council sends their regards, I assume? Along with strongly worded requests for the return of property?"

Several nobles shifted uncomfortably. The frost-skinned woman's rings clinked faster. A younger vampire with shadows clinging to his jacket actually flinched. The council head's smile remained fixed, though frost crept into her tone. "Desperate times call for desperate measures."

Before I could press further, a gaunt vampire with ink-stained fingers materialized at my elbow, managing to look both imperious and nervous as he cleared his throat. "Before we proceed, there is the matter of documentation." He produced an ornate scroll case from his robes and unfurled what appeared to be several feet of parchment across the crystal table. The golden ink of official seals and elaborate calligraphy caught the light.

"This is our non-disclosure agreement and comprehensive liability waiver," the bureaucrat explained, compulsively aligning the sides of the parchment. "All those who engage in work of any type on our premises must sign." He gestured at the document with a flourish.

I glanced at Evander, then at Morana, arching an eyebrow in silent question. Evander's face remained carefully neutral, though I caught the slight twitch at the corner of his mouth.

Curiosity got the better of me. I leaned forward, scanning the elaborate script. "'The signatory hereby waives all rights to compensation for blood sacrifice, accidental exsanguination, unintended vampiric bonding, injuries due to torpor, damages from becoming lost in the crypts or from the denizens in the crypts, psychic hemorrhaging...' Really?" I read further, my eyebrows climbing higher. "'Exclusions include but are not limited to: pre-existing curses, hereditary prophecies, and any damage resulting from third party contracts initiated prior to signing'?"

I laughed. The sound echoed off the chamber walls, making several nobles wince. "You want me to sign paperwork? Let me get this straight. You've stolen artifacts from every major supernatural power, corrupted them with whatever that is." I gestured at the sickly purple-green energy. "And now you're worried about liability?"

The bureaucratic vampire looked scandalized. "It's standard protocol—"

"I think we can dispense with the formalities," Morana cut in smoothly, though her expression suggested someone would be having an unpleasant conversation later. "After all, should the worst occur, the phoenix will simply be reborn." Her smile didn't reach her eyes. "Given the... unique nature of her abilities."

She wasn't wrong, but that was harsh! "Let's get back to the reason you sent for me. What exactly are these desperate times?" I moved closer to the table, examining the artifacts. Evander shadowed my movements, his presence a constant awareness at my back.

The collection before me read like a catalog of supernatural theft, each item pulsing with its own unique magical resonance. They'd managed to offend literally every magical race in existence. Quite the achievement, really. I had to admire their thoroughness, if not their methods. It was like they'd written a how-to guide titled *How to Make Powerful Enemies* and decided to complete it with flourish.

"I see you've been busy," I said to Evander, picking up what appeared to be a fae crystal. "Did you actually check off *anger the fae* on your to-do list, or was that just a happy bonus?"

"We prefer to think of it as aggressive collecting," he replied, the corner of his mouth twitching. "Though I admit, the dragon scales might have been pushing it."

"Might have been?" I arched an eyebrow. "The last time someone stole dragon scales, an entire mountain range became a sea of molten glass. But sure, let's call it aggressive collecting."

"Aggressive collecting," I muttered to myself. *Is that what we're calling theft that could trigger a supernatural war now?*

Grimoires from Eldoria's great libraries lay open, their magical script still smoldering with power despite the purple-green taint that crept along their edges. A wolf pack's sacred moonstone pulsed in rhythm with the lunar cycle, its energy fighting against both the containment spells and the corruption trying to seep into its core.

Deep forest magic radiated from a cluster of bear claws, making the air thick with the scent of pine and wild places. The silvery scars across my collarbone warmed at their proximity, resonating with the same wild energy that had marked me. My fingers rose to trace the three raised lines that crossed from my collarbone to my right shoulder, remembering. A bear shifter, driven to a berserker rage by the loss of his mate, had left these during one of my darker missions. The scars caught the witchlight now, gleaming like moonlight on snow where his primal magic had met my phoenix fire.

I understood that kind of magic in my bones now, knew both its raw destructive power and its capacity for healing. I'd chosen to help rather than harm that day, using my flames to ground him while his grief-fueled strength left these lasting marks. As I reached for the bear claws before me, that old magic recognized me, responding to the echoes of itself etched into my skin. I'd never regretted the choice. Sometimes the most dangerous creatures were simply the most wounded.

I returned my attention to the bear claws. Even their pure essence wavered under the fortress's influence, much like that shifter's power had wavered under the weight of his grief.

Light fractured impossibly through fae crystals, their ancient whispers almost audible in the still air. My eyes caught on a gossamer-thin bottle that seemed to twist in on itself. "Is that bottled fae wind? The kind that can strip flesh from bone and—"

The words died in my throat as I spotted them: dragon scales. Fresh ones. They blazed with internal fire, their edges still raw where they'd been forcibly taken. Somewhere out there, a very angry dragon was missing part of their hide.

Evander shadowed my examination of the artifacts. Each step brought him closer until the chill of his presence offset the heat building beneath my skin. My fire responded to his proximity. Not with the usual defensive surge, but with a curious warmth that spread through my chest. His shadows danced at the edges of my vision, curling protectively around both our feet.

When I turned to face the council, the movement brought us chest to chest. Neither of us stepped back. His cold scent intensified, cutting through the corruption's iron tang. For a moment, the council faded to background noise.

Without thinking, I shifted my weight slightly to make room as he moved to cover my blind spot. It was a warrior's instinct. Protecting a comrade's vulnerabilities. The fact that I'd unconsciously trusted a vampire to guard my back should have terrified me. Instead, I relaxed fractionally into the protective stance even as my mind screamed at the foolishness of it.

Real professional, Ashwing, I thought sourly. *Next you'll be letting him hold your hand.*

The council head descended to the chamber floor, each step precise as a blade stroke. "Perhaps we should discuss the situation in more detail. Privately." Her gaze flickered between Evander and me, noting our proximity with sharp interest.

I caught Evander's minute head shake. A warning so subtle another immortal might have missed it. His hand drifted toward mine. He caught himself, fingers curling into a fist at his side. The red-haired vampire from the second tier leaned forward again, his nostrils flaring as if scenting the tension between us.

"As you wish," I said, matching the council head's pleasant tone. "I'm dying to hear how this all makes perfect sense."

The frost-skinned woman's rings kept turning, faster now, their gemstones catching the light like worried eyes.

The sharp-featured young noble flinched at my choice of words. The council head's smile turned predatory. "If you'll follow me?"

As we walked, reality itself seemed to fray at the edges. My skin crawled with phantom sensations, and each breath felt like swallowing shards of glass. Whatever they'd done, whatever they were dealing with, it was bad enough to make them risk the wrath of every major supernatural power.

The question was: Did they want me to fix it, or did they have other designs?

And why did Evander's obvious concern for my safety make me feel both stronger and more vulnerable at the same time?

Whatever had the vampire nobles this unsettled, I had a feeling I wasn't going to like the explanation. My shoulder brushed against Evander's as we walked. In the heart of the viper's den, I should have been cataloging escape routes and counting enemies. Instead, I was hyperaware of how his shadows curled protectively around both our feet and how my own fire had stopped trying to burn them away.

CHAPTER 3
A STUDY IN CORRUPTION

ADARA

WHEN WE REACHED OUR DESTINATION, THE vampires ushered me into a study that would have made any self-respecting gothic novel proud. Though I had to wonder if vampires had an interior decorator whose entire philosophy was "more shadows, more velvet." Floor-to-ceiling bookshelves groaned under the weight of ancient tomes, their spines bearing titles in languages that made my eyes water just looking at them. The air held that distinct chill unique to vampire spaces, along with the musty sweetness of old parchment and an acrid tang that burned like liquid lightning against my tongue.

A massive ebony desk dominated the space, covered in hastily shuffled maps and documents. But my gaze was drawn to the window beyond, rough-hewn through thick stone. What I saw through it made my phoenix fire stir uneasily beneath my skin.

From this vantage point, the sickly glow I'd noticed earlier was impossible to miss. It pulsed on the horizon, casting strange shadows even at this distance. The councilor made no attempt to close the heavy velvet curtains, which told me this view was entirely intentional. I also suspected the window was a recent addition to the space. Evander shifted closer to me, his shoulder nearly brushing mine. Warmth flooded through me at his nearness, defying his vampiric chill. His shadows reached for me when he thought no one was looking, just as they had in the entrance hall. Such a curious vampire.

"As you can see," Morana said, gesturing to the window. Power emanated from her in waves that demanded submission. Her silver-streaked dark hair caught the portal's sickly light, and frost crystallized in delicate patterns along the edges of her high cheekbones. The air stilled around her, as if winter itself held its breath in her presence. "We face an unusual situation."

"That's one way to put it." I moved closer to the glass, studying the unnatural light. "Another would be we've got a glowing portal consuming our territory, but I suppose that lacks a certain diplomatic flair." The portal's energy made my ancient power coil tighter, like a snake preparing to strike.

I tried to recall if I'd ever seen something like this before, but to no avail. My memories of prior incarnations were unpredictable. Some lives faded completely, others lingered in fragments. A face, a feeling, a lesson learned. The big things always stayed: Wars. Famines. Betrayals. But the personal moments? Those surfaced when they wanted to, not when I called for them. A burden or a blessing, I still wasn't sure which.

"We prefer to think of it as an opportunity," a new voice said from the doorway.

I turned to find another vampire entering. Male this time, all angles and eyes that held no trace of humor. His perfectly pressed clothes and calculating gaze reminded me of the ambitious nobles I'd seen at the council meeting, the ones who measured everything in terms of power gained or lost. He moved to stand beside the councilor, their unified front hardly subtle. Great. Because what this situation really needed was another vampire with delusions of grandeur.

"An opportunity," I repeated flatly. "That's what we're calling holes in reality these days? Tell me, do you also call plagues population control opportunities?"

"Councilor Thane," Evander murmured, introducing the newcomer. His tone was respectful, but I caught the slight tension in his voice, the way his shadows curled protectively closer to where I stood. Interesting. Very interesting.

Thane's smile didn't reach his eyes. "The portal presents unique learning possibilities—"

"The portal," I cut in, "is leaking corruption into your lands. Unless death and decay are the unique possibilities you're hoping for?" The metallic taste in the air grew stronger, reminding me uncomfortably of battlefields I'd seen in past lives. Some opportunities came with prices too steep to calculate.

Morana shot Thane a subduing look before turning back to me, the temperature plummeting around her until frost gathered in spiraling patterns along the edges of her crimson robes. The display of power wasn't subtle: each breath now visible in the suddenly frigid air, ice crystals dancing in her wake as she moved. Now that was an interesting power, wielded with the casual confidence of decades. Centuries maybe? "What Councilor Thane means is that we hope to understand the portal's nature before taking action. With your expertise, of course."

Of course. Because nothing said we want to understand something quite like stealing magical artifacts from every major supernatural race. I crossed my arms, waiting. Behind me, I felt Evander shift closer, his presence a solid anchor against the portal's unsettling pull. His darkness coiled like silk around my legs, a subtle gesture that felt almost... protective? No, that couldn't be right. We were temporary allies at best, no matter how my traitorous body seemed to gravitate toward his.

The councilor glided to the desk, selecting a particular scroll from the mess of documents. The parchment hummed with familiar magic: Mage's Council craftsmanship, if I wasn't mistaken. "We've gathered considerable research materials—"

"Stolen," I corrected. "You've stolen considerable research materials. Let's not dress up theft in misleading terms."

"Acquired through necessary means," Morana countered smoothly, "given the urgency of the situation. This one addresses Mage's research into portals. You might want to start here."

I raised an eyebrow. "And what situation would that be? Because right now all I'm seeing is a portal you're suspiciously interested in studying rather than closing."

The temperature in the room dropped several degrees. Thane's expression hardened, but Morana merely smiled. It was not a comforting expression. In fact, it reminded me distinctly of a desert cobra I'd once met... somewhere? The cobra had been more trustworthy.

"Perhaps," she said, "you need a better view to understand our perspective. Uncomfortable though it may be."

I had a feeling I wasn't going to like their definition of perspective. But then I rarely liked vampire definitions of anything. They tended to involve an awful lot of blood and questionable ethics. *Brace yourself, Adara.*

Morana led our little procession down through the fortress depths, each level darker and colder than the last. Evander kept pace beside me while Thane followed. I didn't miss how Evander had positioned himself between me and the other vampire, his movements subtle but deliberate.

The corruption deepened with each descending step. The air grew viscous and heavy, like breathing through oil.

"Your fortress's ambiance is really something," I muttered to Evander. "Nothing says welcome quite like descending into ever-darker pits of doom."

His lips twitched. "We do try to maintain certain standards."

We emerged from the fortress through a hidden door at its base, stepping onto a narrow path that wound down into a ravine separating vampire territory from human lands. The distant portal's light cast everything in putrid hues, a nauseating blend of decay and poison. The light grew brighter as we descended. Dead vegetation crunched under our feet, gray and twisted into unnatural shapes that made my stomach turn. The silence pressed against my ears like a physical thing, broken only by our footsteps and the subtly wrong hum of the portal's energy. My flames flickered beneath my skin, responding to... something.

"Cheerful place," I muttered. "Really brings out the whole impending doom aesthetic you're going for. Though I have to say, the twisted death garden is a bit on the nose, even for vampires."

"The corruption began nine moons ago," Morana said, ignoring my comment.

"Nine moons," I repeated, thinking back to the recent disturbances I'd sensed in other realms. A pattern started forming in my mind. "That would coincide with the winter solstice."

"Yes," Morana confirmed. "When the darkness of the night peaked. We first noticed it as a mere shimmer in the air, barely visible. Within days, we realized it continued to expand. The impacts were small at first. A few dead plants, some discolored water. Then..."

She gestured to a dead raven at our feet, its feathers bent and twisted. More birds littered the path ahead, as if they'd fallen mid-flight. At the edge of the containment circle, a small pool of water caught the portal's light, its surface sheened with an oily rainbow that swirled to an unseen wind.

"We tried everything within our power," Morana continued. "Blood magic, ancient rites, even attempts to drain its energy. Each failure only made it stronger."

"Which is why you needed the artifacts," I said, understanding dawning. "You're trying to combine different styles of magic."

"The Mage's scrolls suggest it's the only way," Thane

said. "Each race's magic alone isn't enough to close a portal."

I watched another dead bird fall from the sky, its wings already beginning to twist. They were right about one thing: this was getting worse by the hour. Evander's hand brushed mine, so briefly I might have imagined it, but the contact steadied me against the portal's increasing wrongness.

"Fine," I said. I hated every word. "I'll help. But I do it my way."

Morana gestured as we rounded a bend in the path. I stopped short, my breath catching in my throat.

The portal hung in the air like a tear in reality itself, its edges jagged and pulsing with that sickly light. But it wasn't the portal that made my ancient power stir uneasily within me. It was what it was doing to the area around it.

Reality warped inward toward the portal's center, causing a gentle distortion that pulled at me, almost as if it possessed its own gravity. The air itself twisted into impossible shapes, as if reality had decided to take up interpretive dance. Not the elegant kind, either. More like the 'had too much wine at a fae feast' variety. I'd seen more stable patterns in a drunken dragon's flight path. The ground beneath the portal had turned a flat, lifeless gray that spread slowly outward in veins through the soil. The air carried a metallic taste that reminded me of blood and ozone. And there was something else. Something that tugged at memories of catastrophe and sacrifice from lives long past.

"Well," I said, fighting to keep my voice light, "that's definitely not supposed to be there."

"Our thoughts exactly," Thane said dryly.

Morana moved closer to the portal's edge. Closer than any sane person should. "We've established a safe perimeter," she said, gesturing to a series of runes carved into the rock. "Though our containment efforts have proven... challenging."

I studied the runes, recognizing the precise magical signature of the Mage's Council. No wonder they'd stolen the Council's scrolls. They'd been borrowing the Council's methods. The vampires had etched the containment circle into the ravine walls with admirable precision, but even I could see it was failing. Each rune was carved with painstaking exactitude. Because apparently, even when facing imminent doom, proper penmanship was non-negotiable. The etched lines pulsed weakly, their power fading against the portal's constant drain.

Each rune formation followed classical containment theory: layered circles of power connected by binding sigils that should create a resonant barrier against magical anomalies. But the vampires had done something I'd never seen before, weaving their blood magic through the traditional framework. Dark veins of power pulsed between the original runes, crimson energy trying to reinforce the failing wards. The combination should have been impossible. Blood magic typically rejected other magical systems like oil refusing to mix with water. Someone here had a deep understanding of magical theory, or perhaps just enough desperation to ignore the normal rules.

Was that Evander? Was that why he'd been assigned to help me?

I crouched to examine the modifications more closely. The distortion in the air made my skin crawl, but I ignored it. "You've tied the blood magic directly into your fortress's ward network," I said, tracing a finger along one of the hybrid sigils. The discordant vibration of competing magical systems sent pins and needles up my arm.

"Clever, using your existing power structure to amplify the containment field. But that's also why it's failing so quickly. The portal's corruption isn't just attacking the containment circle. It's feeding back through your entire ward network." I pointed to where the corruption had already breached their perimeter. "Your containment is breaking down. How long since you carved these runes?"

"Two days," Evander said quietly. His shadows reached toward the corruption, then recoiled as if burned. The gesture seemed unconscious, but it spoke volumes about how wrong this all was.

I turned to stare at him. "Two days?" A chill ran down my spine. This was wrong. This was all wrong.

"Hence our concern," Morana said. "And our... continued acquisition of additional resources."

Right. And I was just another of those resources. *Lucky me.* Because when magic starts breaking down at unprecedented rates, the obvious solution is to steal more magic. That couldn't possibly go wrong. It's not like I'd seen exactly that kind of thinking destroy an entire civilization before. Except... had I? The memory danced just out of reach. It left behind a sense of impending disaster.

I stepped closer to the portal, staying just outside the containment circle. Reality buckled here, the fabric of existence wearing thin, making my phoenix fire surge and retreat like waves against a hostile shore. This close, I could feel the portal's hunger. A constant pull that seemed to tug at more than just the physical world. It wanted something. Or maybe it was leaking something? Either way, the fact that I couldn't tell was deeply concerning.

Evander moved with me, his presence steady at my back. His shadows stretched between us and the portal, a dark barrier against the corruption, though whether he was trying to shield me or himself, I couldn't tell. Was he worried I'd trip and fall into the portal, destroying their hopes that I'd solve the puzzle? Regardless, the gesture stirred something in my chest. A warmth that had no place in this cold discussion of power and corruption.

"Show me what you've tried so far," I said, forcing myself to focus. "Everything. Including whatever you did with those artifacts you conveniently acquired."

Councilors Morana and Thane exchanged a look that set off every warning bell I possessed.

Oh yes, there was definitely something they weren't telling me. The question was: Would I live long enough to figure out what? And why did the way Evander tensed at their exchange make me think he might be wondering the same thing?

As we turned to head back into the fortress, I caught Evander watching me. For a moment our eyes met, and I saw my own concerns reflected in his gaze. Whatever game the council was playing, neither of us was willing to be just another piece on their board.

But could we trust each other enough to survive whatever came next?

CHAPTER 4

SHADOWS AND STOLEN MAGIC

ADARA

THE JOURNEY FROM THE PORTAL SITE BACK INTO the fortress felt like descending into a pit of vipers: beautiful, deadly, and all too aware of our presence. The distortion I'd sensed at the portal dimmed as we moved deeper underground, but it didn't go away. My magic pulsed beneath my skin, responding to the corruption. To Evander's continued proximity. Both pulled at something deep in my core.

"Now," Councilor Morana said smoothly. Her words broke the charged silence. "We'll show you to where you'll be working." Her tone carried the same false sweetness I'd heard countless times, but underneath it lay something harder, more desperate.

Evander's shadows twisted through the air as we descended. They darkened the space around us. Each time they passed near me, my power stirred in recognition. Instead of the expected revulsion between our opposing natures, his proximity sent shivers of awareness through my core.

Morana led us to a cave mouth I hadn't noticed before, partially hidden behind an outcropping where corruption had leached the rock to a lifeless gray. The entrance had been worked into a proper doorway, more runes carved around its frame. These I recognized as vampire blood magic. Wards meant to keep something out rather than in. The ancient power embedded in the stone sent warning signals cascading through my body, my magic coiling tight in my chest. The wards' pattern was familiar from my studies of First Age magics. Their twisted resonance made bile rise in my throat.

We stepped through the cave's opening into a small space with no discernible path forward. Morana traced a complex sigil in the air and a section of rock face shimmered, revealing the hidden entrance. Deep gouges surrounding the opening marked failed containment attempts. Scorch marks stained the ceiling. A wave of corrupted energy slammed into me, and my power writhed in instinctive defense. The wrongness had wormed its way even into the protective wards, their purpose warped into something that set my teeth on edge. "Our primary research location," she explained, her voice carrying a hint of pride that made my jaw clench. "We positioned it here to monitor the portal's effects directly."

I forced my breathing to steady as I noted the positioning, close enough to study the phenomenon, yet shielded by layers of rock and wards. My fingers twitched against my will as I gestured toward the barriers. "Smart. Using the natural formation as an additional barrier." My eyes caught Thane's reaction. Not just a subtle smirk, but a predatory gleam that transformed his aristocratic features into something ancient and dangerous. He stood straighter, chest swelling with pride, and calculated interest flickered in his gaze as it moved between me and Evander. The hairs on my arms rose as I watched Thane's satisfaction. This wasn't just about containing a threat for him. Thane saw opportunity in this chaos.

"Necessary," Evander corrected quietly, stepping closer until his arm nearly brushed mine. The air between us charged with unspoken tension. "After our first chamber was... compromised."

The way he said *compromised* made me wonder what horrors lay ahead.

We stepped through the newly opened entrance and into a chamber that sent every magical instinct I possessed into high alert. Vampire architecture had transformed the natural cave into something that defied conventional geometry. Obsidian pillars twisted upward at impossible angles, their surfaces etched with runes that shifted when I wasn't looking directly at them. The corruption was stronger here, coating my tongue with a taste like blood mixed with grave dirt.

I forced myself to breathe through my mouth as I took in the room's contents. My fire pressed against my skin, responding to the layers of magic that saturated the space. Above us, crystal formations caught the light from the lamps positioned around the chamber, their naturally perfect geometries warped by the portal's influence.

"This," Thane said, spreading his arms with the theatrical flair of a curator unveiling his masterpiece, "is where we've been studying the portal's unique properties."

His eyes gleamed with an unsettling intensity as he watched me take in the room.

The walls were lined with familiar artifacts which must have been transferred from the council chambers while we'd been touring. Each piece sang with its own magical signature. The cacophony set my teeth on edge. My years of training helped me identify individual voices in the chaos. The deep resonance of earth crystals, the sharp clarity of fae workings, the primal power of dragon-crafted items. But here, corrupted by the portal's influence, their songs had become a discordant shriek of power eating itself.

In the middle of the room stood a long table that told its own story of desperation and escalation. I moved along it slowly, reading the progression of their experiments like a funeral dirge. They'd started conservatively enough with traditional containment methods: the Mage's Council's tried and tested wards and bindings. When those failed, they'd moved to elemental magic, trying to use earth crystals to ground and neutralize the corruption. The dragon scales came next, their raw power twisted into increasingly desperate attempts to burn away the wrongness. Each failure was marked by scorch marks and magical residue that made my fire recoil.

As I reached for one of the fae crystals, Evander's hand caught my wrist. Cool fingers against my fire-warmed skin.

"Wait," he said. "This one's unstable. The corruption's altered its nature."

I arched an eyebrow at him, though I didn't pull away.

"Protecting the dangerous phoenix from harming herself? How thoughtful."

His lips quirked. "Perhaps I'm protecting the crystal from you. I understand your power has a way of... amplifying things."

The moment shattered as one of the nearby dragon scales pulsed with angry red light. Evander's shadows surged forward instinctively as he pulled me behind him, his body shielding mine as the scale's energy lashed out. My magic thundered within me, responding to the threat and, in ways I didn't want to examine, to his protective gesture as his shadows contained the burst of power before it could ignite the other artifacts.

"I see you've been trying to combine different magical sources," I said, forcing myself to focus on the larger threat. "How many researchers have you lost in the attempt?"

The silence that followed was all the answer I needed. Councilors Morana and Thane exchanged a look that spoke volumes about what they weren't saying.

I eyed the dragon scale warily. Sarcasm made an excellent mask for suspicion. "Well," I said, voice bright with false cheer, "at least you've managed to create the world's most expensive paperweight collection. Congratulations."

Thane's eyes narrowed, a flash of something dark crossing his features. His fangs gleamed briefly. "This is no laughing matter, Lady Ashwing."

"Oh, I'm aware," I replied, my smile turning sharp as my power coiled tight with tension. "But sometimes I have to laugh to keep from setting everything on fire. Speaking of which—" I gestured to a particularly nasty scorch mark on the ceiling. "I'm guessing that wasn't part of your interior design plan?"

Evander ran a hand through his hair. His carefully maintained aristocratic facade cracked, revealing exhaustion and something that looked uncomfortably like fear. This close, I could see the strain in his features, the toll that the portal's corruption was taking on him.

Morana stepped forward, her composure barely masking her irritation. "We've made significant progress in understanding the portal's nature, which Lord Nightshade will be available to discuss with you."

"Mmhmm." I moved to examine a scroll covered in hastily scrawled notes. "And by 'significant progress' you mean we've figured out sixteen new ways to blow ourselves up?"

Evander cleared his throat. "Perhaps we should focus on what we've learned, rather than our... setbacks." His voice carried a warning note meant for me alone.

I turned to face him, noting the careful neutrality in his expression. But his eyes told a different story. Concern warring with something deeper, more personal.

"Alright," I said, setting down the scroll and crossing my arms. "Enlighten me. What exactly have you learned about this portal that was worth risking an all-out war with every major supernatural faction?"

Morana gestured to a series of diagrams pinned to the wall. "The portal appears to be a tear in the fabric of reality itself. It's not just a gateway to another realm. It's a wound in the very essence of our world."

The portal's energy pulsed through the chamber, a dark answer to her words. I watched in horror as a moth that had somehow found its way inside flew too close to one of the corrupted crystals. Its wings twisted into impossible shapes before it crumbled to ash.

"Charming," I muttered. Nausea clawed at my throat. *Get it together, Adara.* "And you thought poking at it with stolen magic was the best solution?"

Thane bristled, his fangs flashing. "Binding magic, and we had no choice. The corruption was spreading too quickly. We must understand it before we can hope to contain it." Something in his tone sent warning bells ringing through my mind. There was an eagerness there that went beyond mere scientific curiosity.

I raised an eyebrow. "And it never occurred to you that maybe, just maybe, throwing more magic at a magical problem might make things worse?"

"We took precautions..." Morana began.

"Clearly," I interrupted, gesturing to the scarred walls. My fire flared with my anger. Evander's shadows surged in response, trying to temper my reaction. "Top-notch safety protocols you've got here. Really inspiring confidence."

Morana's eyes flashed with barely suppressed anger, and I wondered if I'd gone too far. "We did what was necessary to protect our territory. And by extension, the human lands beyond."

Wait, what? I snorted. I definitely hadn't gone far enough. "Oh please, spare me the altruistic act."

Silence fell over the chamber, the tension between us palpable. The portal's corruption seemed to feed on it, its virulent energy coiling tighter around us. I could feel the weight of centuries of vampire pride warring with raw desperation. Even Evander's shadows had gone still, like the moment before a storm breaks.

Evander stepped forward, close enough that the chill emanating from his body made my fire surge in response. "Lady Ashwing," he said. Gone was the carefully crafted diplomatic mask, replaced by something raw and urgent that tightened my throat. "I understand your frustration. But please, hear us out. The situation is..." He hesitated, and I watched his composure crack even further. "... It's more complex than it appears."

His hand rose to his hair again. I noted how the witchlight caught the tension in his shoulders, the subtle tremor in his normally steady hands. This wasn't the calculated vulnerability of a vampire noble playing politics. But was it fear for himself, or for his people?

"The portal," he continued, voice dropping to barely above a whisper, "it's not just corrupting the land. It's affecting our very nature." He raised his hand, attempting to trace a basic blood sigil. A demonstration. The magic sputtered and died like a candle in a storm. The failure caused him physical pain, a flash of agony crossing his features before he could mask it.

"What do you mean?"

"Our powers, our connection to blood magic, it's weakening." His voice roughened with suppressed emotion. "At first, we thought it was just the proximity to the portal, but..." He gestured to a series of maps on the wall that I hadn't noticed before, each marked with dates and measurements. The progression was clear even from where I stood. "The effect is spreading. Every day, our connection to our own magic grows weaker. Some of the younger vampires..." He broke off, jaw clenching.

"They're losing their powers entirely," I finished, the pieces clicking horribly into place. The desperate experiments, the stolen artifacts, the mounting tension in vampire territory. It wasn't just about containing the portal. "You're afraid it's going to strip away your vampiric nature completely."

Well. That explained the desperation.

Our eyes met, and for a heartbeat, the rest of the chamber ceased to exist. The portal's corruption, the political machinations, the ancient prejudices between our kinds. None of it seemed to matter in the face of this revelation.

The moment shattered as Thane cleared his throat, reminding us we weren't alone.

The calculating glint in his eyes confirmed what I'd suspected.

Whatever game he was playing, I had a feeling Evander and I were both meant to be pieces on his board. I'd been around politics long enough to know that pawns rarely survived to see the endgame.

"I'll do what I can to help," I said finally, tearing my gaze away from Evander. Each word felt like a powerfully weighted vow. "For the sake of the realms, not just your coven. But I need to see everything. No half-truths or conveniently omitted details. If you want my help, I need to know exactly what we're dealing with."

Morana and Thane excused themselves, their departure carrying the careful dignity of predators pretending not to retreat. Like cats pretending they'd meant to miss that jump. Everything was a production with vampires.

Evander and I settled in to examine the research. I couldn't shake the feeling that I was missing something vital, some piece of the puzzle that would make sense of Thane's smug satisfaction and Morana's barely contained anxiety. Sometimes the most dangerous mysteries were the ones that made you question everything you thought you knew about yourself and your enemies.

CHAPTER 5

FIRE AND SHADOW, BOUND IN INK

ADARA

SLEEP ELUDED ME LONG AFTER EVANDER HAD shown me to my chambers, my skin still alive with sensation where his fingers had lingered. Every time I closed my eyes, I saw the intensity in his gaze, felt the electric charge when we'd touched. The memory of his shadows curling around my fire made me shiver. My flame-script remembered, even when I tried not to. Dangerous. Impossible. And apparently, inevitable.

The sunset found me descending the winding path to the research chamber for what felt like the hundredth time in a week, trying to focus on our mission rather than the lingering effects of last night's encounter. After I'd arrived at the fortress, I'd taken up Evander's nighttime schedule, which contributed to my insomnia. The fortress's atmosphere had grown heavier, more oppressive, since I'd started trying to understand what made the portal tick. The very stones pulsed with the blight, the metallic tang of it coating my tongue with each breath.

The research chamber had evolved from its initial

chaos into something approaching organized disaster. If there was a filing system at work here, it seemed to be "sort by likelihood to explode." Sub-categories included "things that go bump in the night." I'd seen more orderly arrangements in dragon hoard caves, and those were organized by whatever shiny object caught their attention last. At least the vampires had labeled everything in perfect calligraphy. Heaven forbid supernatural catastrophe arrive without proper documentation.

The chamber itself hummed with power straining at its edges. My phoenix-fire wards cast rippling patterns of warmth and light across the walls, their glow a stark contrast to the perpetual shadows that clung to the fortress's architecture. Fae crystals hummed discordantly near the eastern wall, their song clashing with the deeper resonance of dragon scales. Bear claws and wolf pelts occupied their own corner, their primal energy grounding the more volatile magics. The vampire artifacts, ancient bloodstones and shadow-wrapped relics, pulsed with a hungry darkness that made my fire stir uneasily beneath my skin.

I paused at the threshold, struck by how the space reflected our growing understanding of each other. Evander's precise organization meshed with my more intuitive approach. The result somehow worked despite breaking half the traditional rules of magical storage.

Heat crept up my neck. I pushed it aside, focusing instead on the complex web of warning spells we'd woven throughout the chamber. After yesterday's near disaster with the resonating crystals, we'd added three new layers of protective enchantments. The air shimmered with overlapping fields of power, my fire wards intertwining with Evander's shadow barriers in a way that should have been impossible.

A flicker of movement caught my eye, one of the smaller artifacts shifting slightly on its shelf, responding to the portal's distant pulse. The corruption was growing stronger, its influence reaching deeper into the fortress with each passing day. Time was slipping away. We still didn't understand what we were dealing with, let alone how to stop it.

I moved to my usual workstation where dozens of ancient texts lay open to various passages about magical anomalies and realm disturbances. The scent of old parchment mingled with the metallic tang of decay. Scholarly and vaguely threatening in equal measure. Perfect for a vampire's research chamber, truly.

But as I reached for the text I'd been studying last night, my hand hesitated. The diagrams I'd been puzzling over blurred, and my flame-script pulsed with distant recognition. A pattern I should recognize if I could just...

"Lady Ashwing." Councilor Morana's voice hit me like a bucket of ice water. She stood in the doorway, her silver-streaked dark hair arranged in elaborate coils that seemed to absorb light. Unlike many of the younger vampires, she maintained her usual grace, though I noticed the slight tremor in her left hand as she ran her fingers along one of her hanging braids. "I trust your research progresses?"

Behind her, Thane's angular features showed none of the strain I'd observed in other vampires, but the tic in his jaw betrayed his agitation. His crimson robes, typically pristine, showed subtle signs of wear, evidence that even the highest-ranking vampires weren't immune to the corruption's effects.

"As well as can be expected," I replied carefully. Thane's eyes darted to the artifacts we'd cataloged. His interest in certain pieces had grown more obvious over the past week, particularly the items capable of storing or transferring power. "Though perhaps the council could assist by sharing more details about the portal's initial discovery?"

A third figure emerged from the shadows. Lady Elena, her frost-white skin nearly luminescent in the chamber's magical light. Her hands never stopped moving, twisting her rings in an endless nervous dance. Of all the council members, she seemed most affected by the corruption, her glamour magics, which should have been powerful, failing noticeably. The illusion that should have masked her age flickered intermittently, revealing glimpses of ancient features before snapping back into place.

"We've provided all relevant information," Thane said smoothly, though I caught the sharp look Morana shot him. Interesting. Not all the council members were playing from the same grimoire, it seemed.

"Have you?" I moved to adjust one of the containment wards, using the motion to study their reactions. "Including why you chose this particular location for your... research facility?"

Elena's rings clinked faster. Thane's expression darkened. Only Morana maintained her perfect composure, although the temperature around her dropped several degrees while fingers of frost snaked across the tops of her shoes. "The location was chosen for its natural defensive properties," she said. "Nothing more."

The lie hung in the air between us, as obvious as the corruption's metallic taste on my tongue. Before I could press further, a familiar presence materialized in the doorway. Evander's arrival sent an immediate ripple through the chamber, both magical and political. The council members shifted subtly, their dynamics changing with the appearance of the noble.

"Lord Nightshade," Morana acknowledged, her tone carrying layers of meaning I couldn't quite decipher. "How... fortunate you're here. Perhaps you can help persuade Lady Ashwing to focus on containment rather than historical inquiries?"

Evander met my eyes briefly, a wealth of unspoken communication passing between us. The council's scrutiny over the past week had grown increasingly pointed, their questions more specific. Each day brought us closer to the moment they'd force our hand, and we still hadn't uncovered the truth.

"I believe all avenues of research have merit," he said diplomatically, moving to stand near my workstation. His shadows swirled around his feet, flitting around my own feet and up my legs before they pulled back. My flame-script flared beneath my skin at the brief contact, an unwanted recognition I couldn't suppress. I hoped the others didn't notice. "The historical context could tell us what we're actually dealing with."

"Indeed." Thane's smile didn't reach his eyes. "Though perhaps some historical records are best left... undisturbed."

The threat in his words was subtle but clear. Even Elena stilled at his tone, and Morana's perfect mask cracked slightly. The council was fracturing under the corruption's influence, old alliances straining as their powers waned.

Watching vampire nobles try to maintain their dignity while their world crumbled was like watching peacocks attempt to strut through a hurricane: impressive dedication to appearances, if somewhat missing the point of impending disaster. At least their robes still billowed dramatically during arguments. Priorities, I supposed. I wondered if they practiced their robe-billowing in front of mirrors, then remembered the obvious flaw in that plan. No wonder they all looked so frustrated; centuries of perfecting their dramatic exits and they couldn't even check if they were doing it right.

One of the fae crystals suddenly flared with sickly light, its usual moonlit glow shot through with threads of the purple-green energy we'd observed in the portal. The crystal's song turned discordant, setting my teeth on edge. Before anyone could react, the dragon scales began to resonate in response, their usual fire darkening to an unnatural hue.

I moved instinctively, my phoenix fire surging forth to contain the magical backlash. Evander's shadows joined my efforts without hesitation, our powers weaving together to create a barrier around the destabilizing artifacts. The ease of our cooperation drew sharp looks from the council members, but I was too focused on the immediate threat to care. Evander pulled a pouch from his coat and poured a line of black salt around the fae crystals, and they settled down for the moment. Only then could we drop our joint shielding.

"Fascinating," Thane murmured, watching the corruption spread through the crystal's structure. "The way it adapts to different magical signatures..."

"Fascinating isn't the word I'd use," I snapped, noting how the corruption seemed to reach for the vampire artifacts next, as if drawn to their innate darkness. "This is the third incident this week, and they're getting worse."

Elena drifted closer to the encircled crystals, her glamour flickering rapidly now. "The resonance patterns... they're similar to what we observed in the younger vampires when their powers first began to fade." Her rings sparked with failing protection spells as she gestured to the crystals. "See how it seeks out the strongest sources of power?"

I exchanged a look with Evander. Hearing it confirmed by a council member was significant.

Before we could press further, a commotion erupted in the corridor. Two younger vampires stumbled past the doorway, one supporting the other. The second vampire's skin had taken on a sickly translucence, veins dark and visible beneath the surface in a way that was wrong even for their kind.

Morana moved to close the door, but not before I glimpsed a third vampire running to help carry their fallen comrade. The blight was spreading faster than anyone wanted to admit, working through the ranks from youngest to eldest. Only those with the strongest innate powers, like the council members, seemed able to resist, and even they were showing strain.

"This is why we need results," Morana said, her tone sharp despite her perfect composure. "Not historical research or theoretical discussions. The corruption spreads and our people suffer."

I turned back to my workstation, pulling out the diagram that had caught my attention earlier. "These aren't just theoretical discussions," I said, spreading the ancient parchment across my desk. "Look at these energy patterns. The way the corruption propagates through different magical frequencies... it's not random. It's almost like..."

"Like it's been designed to target specific types of magic," Evander finished, leaning over my shoulder to study the diagrams. His nearness made my fire stir beneath my skin, momentarily distracting me from the gravity of our discovery. "Starting with the most vulnerable and working its way up through the magical hierarchy."

If the portal's corruption was indeed engineered rather than natural, it meant someone had deliberately targeted the vampire community. Someone with intimate knowledge of how their powers worked and how to systematically dismantle them.

A muscle ticked in Evander's jaw, the only outward sign of his distress, but I'd learned to read him well enough over the past week to recognize the tension thrumming through him.

"If you'll excuse me," he said, his voice carefully controlled, "I need to check on something." His eyes met mine briefly, carrying a weight of meaning I was learning to interpret. This wasn't just any errand. He was going to check on his sister.

The council members exchanged loaded glances at his departure. "Such devotion," Thane remarked, his tone just shy of mocking. "One might almost forget his... previous defiance against the coven, seeing him so dedicated to our cause now."

I kept my expression neutral, though my fire stirred at his implied threat. Through careful conversations over late-night research sessions, I'd learned fragments of Evander's history with the coven, enough to guess there was more to his current status than simple political maneuvering.

I turned back to the artifacts, making a show of adjusting containment wards while keeping one eye on the council members. Their dynamic had shifted subtly with Evander's departure. Elena paced near the door, her steps restless and uneven. Morana's perfect posture held an edge of strain now, like ice about to crack. And Thane... Thane watched it all with the calculated patience of a predator waiting for prey to tire.

When Evander returned shortly after, I caught the slight shadows under his eyes, the barely perceptible tremor in his usually steady hands. His sister's condition must be deteriorating. She was young, too young by vampire standards, and the corruption was hitting the youngest vampires hardest. My chest tightened.

"The lower levels are reporting increased anomalies," he announced, his voice carrying no hint of his personal distress. "The corruption has intensified again."

"Then perhaps," Thane said smoothly, "it's time we considered more... aggressive containment measures." His gaze lingered meaningfully on the most dangerous artifacts we'd collected.

"No." The word came out sharper than I'd intended,

drawing all eyes to me. "The research clearly shows that adding more power to this unstable magical situation only accelerates the corruption. Unless that's what you're hoping for?"

A heavy silence fell over the chamber. Even Elena's nervous ring-twisting stilled. Calculation flashed behind Thane's eyes before his expression smoothed back into careful neutrality. But I'd seen it, that flicker of purpose that confirmed my growing suspicions about his intentions.

"Perhaps," Morana interjected smoothly, "we should allow Lady Ashwing and Lord Nightshade to continue their research without... interference." The temperature around her dropped further, her words carrying the weight of command despite their diplomatic phrasing. "We have other matters requiring our attention."

As the council members filed out, Thane lingered in the doorway. "Do be careful with those artifacts, Lady Ashwing. Some powers are more... volatile than others." His gaze flickered between Evander and me meaningfully before he disappeared into the shadows of the corridor.

The moment they were gone, I felt some of the tension leave my shoulders. Evander moved closer, ostensibly to examine the diagrams I'd been studying, but I noticed how his shadows automatically reached for my fire, seeking that familiar connection we'd been developing.

"Your sister," I said softly. "How is she?"

His hands stilled on the parchment. "Slipping deeper into torpor. The corruption..." He swallowed hard, another unusually human gesture for him. "Her shadows are almost completely gone now. If we can't stop this—"

"We will. And if we don't, perhaps you need to move her." I covered his hand with mine, ignoring the way my flame-script flared at the contact. "But Evander, what Thane suggested about aggressive containment, I've seen that kind of thinking before. In another life, another civilization. I don't recall the details, but I'm certain it didn't end well."

He turned his hand beneath mine, our fingers intertwining almost of their own accord. His other hand found the silvery claw marks at my collarbone. "These scars... they're from helping someone too, aren't they?" His touch was gentle, questioning. "A shifter, perhaps? The marks have that primal resonance to them."

I nodded, fighting not to shiver at his touch. "A bear shifter. He'd lost his mate and the grief drove him into a berserker rage. I couldn't just let them put him down like a rabid animal." I closed my eyes, remembering. "He was so lost in his pain he couldn't tell friend from foe anymore. But I knew what that kind of grief could do to someone; how it could make even the gentlest soul turn dangerous."

"You chose to help rather than harm," Evander murmured. His fingers followed the silvery lines to my shoulder. "Even knowing the risk."

"Some risks are worth taking." I met his gaze, the weight of unspoken meaning hanging between us.

"It's like trying to catch smoke," I admitted, frustrated. "I know I've seen these patterns before, but the details keep slipping away." I pulled my hand back reluctantly, turning to rifle through another stack of texts. "There's something about the way the corruption spreads, how it's targeting specific magical frequencies—"

I broke off as Evander stepped closer and reached past me for a scroll. The movement brought him firmly into my personal space, his chest nearly brushing my back. His scent surrounded me. Old parchment and winter nights, with something darker beneath that called to the fire in my blood. Focus. I needed to focus on the texts.

"These energy signatures," he said, his voice low and close to my ear. "They're similar to what you showed me yesterday, but there's something else..." His free hand came to rest on the desk beside mine, effectively bracketing me between his arms as we studied the diagrams together.

"You know," I said, forcing lightness into my voice, "you never did tell me how you got stuck with this assignment. Babysitting the dangerous Elemental Phoenix can't have been your first choice."

His soft chuckle stirred my hair. "Hardly a difficult assignment. I've long questioned the council's methods. My father did the same, until we lost him a decade ago. Since then, the council and I have been at odds more often than not."

"Wait." I shifted to face him. "You're a born vampire? Lord Nightshade indeed. I thought that was just one of those pretentious council titles."

"Yes, though we're becoming quite rare. I'm younger than many vampires, just a hundred twenty-eight. The others on the council are all a few hundred plus, usually after living a few decades as a human first. Morana and Thane..." He shook his head. "They're ancient by either standard."

A laugh escaped before I could stop it, and I bit back the sound. When he raised an eyebrow, I explained, "I actually thought you were older. Much older. All that brooding and aristocratic bearing..."

"And you?" he asked, a smile playing at the corners of his mouth. "How many centuries has the phoenix graced us with her presence this incarnation?"

"That's..." I hesitated, oddly self-conscious. "It's complicated. I've been reborn many times, but this round? Not quite twenty years." At his surprised look, I added defensively, "That's a long time for me, relatively speaking. And I don't start as a babe, which is a blessing."

The tension around his eyes eased. "It must be frustrating, starting over each time without full recall of your past existence."

"You have no idea," I sighed. "Imagine having a library full of crucial information, but all the books are in different languages and you can only read random pages at a time."

I forced myself to focus on the scrolls rather than our proximity. This was about research. About saving his sister and his people.

But when I turned my head slightly to point out a particular pattern, I found his face much closer than expected. Our eyes met. My flame-script flared, and I didn't try to hide it. Neither of us looked away.

A sudden second surge of corruption from the fae crystals shattered the moment. We sprang apart and moved as one to contain the magical backlash. Our powers layered together automatically now, shadow and flame creating barriers that neither of us could have managed alone.

The corruption's attack was stronger this time, more

focused. The crystal's song transformed into harsh, discordant notes that grated on my nerves. Purple-green energy writhed against our containment field, probing for weakness. But this surge felt different. Focused. Almost purposeful.

"Evander," I said, my voice tight with concentration, "look at the pattern. It's not random decay anymore. It's—"

"Testing our defenses," he finished, his shadows coiling tighter around my flames. "Like it's learning."

The realization hit us both at the same time. I turned to the diagrams spread across my desk, tracing the progression of energy patterns with unsteady fingers. "These aren't just showing corruption spread. They're showing evolution. The portal isn't just leaking power, it's—"

A thunderous boom shook the fortress, cutting off my words. The very air vibrated, and my flame-script surged in response, phoenix fire rising instinctively to meet the threat even as my stomach lurched. Books tumbled from shelves, artifacts rattled in their containment fields, and the metallic taste of corruption grew overwhelming.

"No," Evander breathed, his face draining of what little color it had. "Not now. Not yet." His shadows writhed, panic bleeding through his control, and I knew he was thinking of his sister, of how little time we had left.

The corruption's purple-green glow seeped through cracks in the stone walls, casting sickly shadows across the chamber. Even the strongest containment wards flickered as waves of disruptive energy pulsed through the fortress. Above us, I could hear the sounds of chaos erupting.

Running feet, shouted orders, the crash of objects falling as vampires' powers failed mid-use.

When the energy surge relented, we were able to focus on picking up the room, for what felt like the thousandth time.

"We need to move faster." I gathered books and scrolls from the floor. "Whatever Thane and his supporters are planning—"

"Will have to wait," Evander cut in sharply. His eyes had gone fully crimson, the strain of maintaining his powers evident in the tight lines around his mouth. "The council will want answers about this surge. They'll be looking for us both."

He was right, but something about the diagrams kept nagging at me. Why couldn't I remember? Something about the way the corruption was evolving, adapting, learning...

"Evander." I caught his arm as he turned to leave, my flame-script pulsing hot at the contact despite the crisis. "Whatever happens next, whatever the council demands, we need to be careful. The portal isn't just a tear in reality anymore. It's becoming something else entirely."

His fingers closed over mine where I gripped his arm, his touch oddly gentle despite the urgency vibrating through him. "Trust goes both ways, Phoenix," he said softly. "Whatever you're remembering, whatever you suspect, you need to share it with me."

Neither of us spoke. There was too much to say. Another boom shook the fortress and we broke apart, but the air between us had changed. We'd made a choice without speaking it.

As we hurried to meet the inevitable summons from the council, the sense of time slipping away clung to me, and not just because of the portal. The corruption was evolving, the council was splintering, and I'd stopped pretending I didn't care whether Evander survived this.

The storm was coming. And here I was, a phoenix who'd died and returned so many times the count had lost meaning, terrified of losing someone I'd known for barely a week.

CHAPTER 6
ARCHIVES
AND ANSWERS
ADARA

T HE COUNCIL CHAMBER'S OPPRESSIVE ATMOSPHERE lingered like a bad dream as we finally escaped hours of circular arguments and thinly veiled threats. I'd seen glaciers move faster than vampire politics. Though I suppose when you're immortal, you can afford to debate comma placement for a century or two.

The taste of stale blood magic coated my tongue, bitter and metallic. Apparently even their bureaucracy needed to taste intimidating.

My fire simmered beneath my skin, irritated by the political posturing while corruption spread through their territory unchecked. Every heartbeat echoed the pulse of the distant portal, a discordant rhythm growing stronger each day. The endless debate about proper procedures while their world crumbled around them was enough to make me want to set the whole chamber ablaze. Which, admittedly, wouldn't have helped our cause.

"Well, that was spectacularly unproductive," I muttered as we emerged into the torch-lit corridor, the massive obsidian doors closing behind us with an ominous thud.

Evander's jaw remained tight with barely contained frustration. "Welcome to Crimson Veil politics. All ceremony and no substance." He glanced around, then lowered his voice. "Though perhaps that's for the best. I have something to show you. Somewhere we might make actual progress."

I raised an eyebrow at his conspiratorial tone but followed as he led us away from the public areas of the fortress. The architecture shifted subtly as we moved deeper into the private wings, the overwhelming Gothic drama giving way to something older, more refined. Shadows grew deeper here, more alive, responding to Evander's presence with an almost sentient awareness. The air grew less oppressive, carrying hints of old parchment and aging wood rather than the copper tang of blood magic that permeated the main halls.

My footsteps echoed differently too, the sound muffled by thick carpets rather than bouncing off cold stone. The temperature dropped steadily as we descended, though not with the artificial chill of vampire magic. This was the natural coolness of spaces buried deep within the fortress's heart. What showed above ground was just the tip of the fortress; its true mass stretched deep into the earth below.

Reaching an intricately carved wooden door, Evander paused, glancing at me as if he were taking my measure before turning the handle and swinging it open. "Welcome to my chambers," he said, gesturing for me to enter.

I stepped inside and warmth wrapped around me like a blanket. Dark wood paneling, velvet draperies, ancient tomes stacked everywhere. The whole space screamed *I've had centuries to cultivate taste and you mortals wouldn't understand.* At least it was warmer than the rest of this ice palace. My flame-script flickered with surprise as I took it in. He'd brought me here. To his private sanctuary. Either he trusted me or he was setting an elaborate trap. My fire couldn't decide which possibility was more dangerous. The collection radiated an energy that called to my own power, making my skin prickle with recognition.

Not a noble's showroom. A sanctuary built over centuries, handed down through generations. A place where Evander could be himself rather than what the Crimson Veil expected. The thought settled uncomfortably in my chest. I didn't want to see him as anything other than a means to an end. Seeing him as a person who'd carved out his own space in a world demanding rigid conformity? That was inconvenient. That was dangerous.

As I ran my fingers along the spines of ancient tomes, memories flickered at the edges of my consciousness. Fragments of other lives, other libraries. The magic within stirred at my touch, recognizing something kindred in my fire, something as old and wild as these carefully preserved pages. I'd seen collections like this before, watched them burn, watched them rise again. How many of my past selves had stood in rooms like this, searching for answers to their own world-ending crises? The thought was both comforting and troubling. Comforting because I'd faced impossible odds before and survived, even if survival meant rebirth. Troubling because I couldn't shake the feeling that I was missing something vital, some crucial piece of knowledge lost between my cycles of death and renewal.

"I see your family has quite the collection," I mused. "Planning on opening a library for the magically mischievous? 'Nightshade's Guide to Nefarious Knowledge' has a nice ring to it. Though your organizational system seems to be chaos with occasional alphabetical aspirations."

Evander's lips quirked in a half-smile. "Hardly. The Nightshade archives are a closely guarded secret. Consider yourself privileged, Adara."

"Oh, I'm positively swooning with gratitude," I drawled, grabbing a particularly thick tome and settling into a high-backed chair that was far more comfortable than it had any right to be. "Should I fan myself dramatically, or is that too cliché even for vampires? Though I have to admit, your furniture clearly didn't get the memo about mandatory discomfort in Gothic architecture."

He chuckled, but didn't rise to my bait. Instead, he plucked an old tome off the shelf and dusted it off. "Let's see what my ancestors have to say about realm wounds and portals that shouldn't exist, shall we?"

We fell into a comfortable rhythm of research, the rustle of pages and occasional murmur of discovery the only sounds breaking the silence. The ancient tomes covered every surface, their spines labeled in the kind of perfect script that suggested someone had spent several centuries perfecting their handwriting. Immortality apparently came with plenty of time for penmanship practice.

I relaxed despite myself in this space, away from the prying eyes and political maneuvering of the coven proper. The warm glow of enchanted lanterns cast a gentle light that was easier on the eyes than the harsh crimson illumination favored by the rest of the fortress. More than that, though, was the unexpected pleasure of working alongside someone who matched my intellectual curiosity.

Evander proved to be a surprisingly adept research partner, his knowledge of ancient languages complementing my own. More than once, I watched him pore over a text, brow furrowed in concentration. The fierce intelligence behind those steel-gray eyes was intriguing. Inconveniently intriguing. His fingers traced lines of text with a scholar's precision that made me wonder what else those elegant hands were capable of. When he murmured translations under his breath, shivers raced down my spine that I told myself were simply due to the chamber's perpetual chill and not the low timbre of his voice.

"Here," he said suddenly, pushing an open book toward me. "This passage mentions a similar phenomenon occurring during the breaking of the Fae realms."

I leaned in, my shoulder brushing his as I scanned the text. The touch sent a shiver through me, one I pointedly ignored. His presence surrounded me, familiar now but no less distracting. "Good catch. The energy patterns described here match what we've been seeing with the portal."

"That was a pivotal moment in history; the reverberations echoed through every realm," Evander mused. "It heralded the great upheaval."

A growing unease settled in my gut. "Which begs the question: What shift are we facing now? And who stands to benefit from it?"

A soft knock interrupted our musings. A young male servant entered, carrying a tray laden with fruits, bread, and wine for me. But it was the way he moved toward Evander that caught my attention. The deliberate grace, the slight bow of his head, the healing bite marks on his exposed neck. This was no ordinary servant. He was a blood servant.

"I thought you both might need refreshment," he said, his voice carrying a demure hint of something I couldn't quite place. "My lady." He somehow found an open spot on the table near me and set the tray down with practiced ease, then turned to Evander. "My lord, would you care to partake?"

The air in the room shifted. I should have looked away. Should have suddenly found the ceiling fascinating, or counted the books on the nearest shelf, or done literally anything other than watch a vampire feed. Instead I sat there like an idiot as Evander took the servant's wrist.

This was the first time I'd witnessed a feeding within these walls. I wanted to excuse myself, but my legs had apparently forgotten how to function. Fantastic. His fangs gleamed in the lamplight before he bit down. The servant's eyes fluttered closed, a soft sigh escaping his lips. My phoenix fire flared low in my core, and I hated myself a little for the reaction. This was a vampire feeding, not a performance for my entertainment. Evander's eyes met mine over the servant's extended arm, crimson bleeding into steel gray. The hunger in his gaze hit me like a physical force.

Watching him like this, all careful control stripped away, I understood why vampires were dangerous in ways that had nothing to do with fangs. My fire stirred in response, and I grabbed my wine glass, desperate for something to do with my hands that wasn't reaching for him.

I gulped and then coughed on my wine. "I trust you're well compensated for your... service?" I asked, trying to keep my voice steady.

The servant smiled as Evander finished, carefully withdrawing his fangs, licking the wounds, and then running a thumb over the puncture marks until they sealed. "More than fairly, my lady. The Crimson Veil provides well for those who serve. My family has lived comfortably for three generations through our contributions to the blood tithe."

The blood servant's devotion stirred uncomfortable memories of other forms of sanctified servitude I'd witnessed across my lives. But there was nothing of the Crimson Veil's usual casual cruelty in Evander's careful handling of the servant, just genuine respect and measured control. His chambers, his conduct, even his research methods spoke of someone trying to balance tradition and progress, duty and personal conviction. The realization made my attraction to him all the more dangerous. Respect was worse than desire. Desire I could burn through. Respect lingered.

The servant's departure left a charged silence in his wake. I became hyperaware of Evander as we returned to our research. The way his fingers lingered on each page, the subtle shift in his scent now that he'd fed, the occasional brush of his sleeve against mine as he reached for another tome. But what we discovered in those ancient texts quickly overshadowed everything else. Hours passed, and our findings grew increasingly disturbing, each discovery darker than what came before. The similarities between historical realm wounds and our current crisis were undeniable, and the implications made even vampire politics seem trivial in comparison.

I rubbed my eyes, fighting the exhaustion clouding my judgment. The words on the ancient pages swam before me, and I could feel my fire flickering erratically beneath my skin, a warning sign I'd been pushing too hard. "This passage confirms what we theorized earlier," I muttered, gesturing to the text before me. "If it's correct, the portal isn't just a tear in reality. It's actively seeking out sources of power."

Evander leaned closer to study the diagrams, his shoulder pressing against mine. Awareness sparked between us, and I caught the way his nostrils flared slightly as well. My power's instability must have made my scent more potent, more tempting. "Which would explain why our abilities are failing first," he said, his voice rougher than usual. "We're the most concentrated source of supernatural energy in the area."

I forced a laugh to hide my growing awareness of our precarious position: me with my defenses weakening, him with his hunger rising. "Congratulations. You've managed to make yourselves look like a giant chum bucket to a parasitic portal." I flashed him a wry smile. "Though I suppose that's rather ironic, coming from a vampire stronghold. How does it feel to be on the other end of the food chain for once?"

His eyes narrowed, a flash of red bleeding into the steel gray. "This is hardly a joking matter, Adara."

"Oh, I'm well aware," I shot back, fatigue making my tone sharper than intended. I stood up and paced, trying to burn off the stress of the moment. "The pressure of saving your entire coven, and also perhaps the entire vampire realm, is just weighing on me a bit."

The silence that followed was heavy, charged with everything we hadn't said. I could feel Evander's gaze on me, intense and searching. When I finally stopped pacing, I met his eyes, and what I saw in them had nothing to do with blood.

"Adara," he began, his voice rough with some emotion I couldn't quite name. "I—"

The room decided to spin. How thoughtful of it. Darkness crept into the edges of my vision, drowning out his words. I reached for something solid as my knees considered mutiny. Very dignified, Ashwing. Evander caught me before I could collapse, his arms steadying me against his chest.

"Are you alright?" Evander asked, concern evident in his voice. "I should have sent for food for you earlier."

I took a step back and waved him off, trying to focus. "I'm fine. Just tired. We've been at this for hours and I—"

The words died in my throat as I caught sight of Evander's face. His usual composure had cracked, revealing a raw hunger that sent a shiver down my spine. His eyes had gone fully crimson, and I could see the sharp points of his fangs as he struggled to maintain control.

"Evander?" I said cautiously, my hand instinctively moving to summon my power.

He shook his head, backing away. "I'm sorry," he ground out. "I thought I could... but being so close to you, your scent, your power... I can't..."

The hunger gnawing at him went deeper than physical need. Primal. Desperate. A need to reclaim the power slipping away from him and his kind. Here I was, a source of blood and power, wrapped in a tasty human-appearing package.

Looking at him stripped of his careful control, my phoenix fire surged in answer, craving his darkness.

For a heartbeat, neither of us moved. The air crackled between us. Want. Need. And something darker that neither of us should have been reaching for.

Then Evander surged forward, closing the distance between us in an instant. His hand tangled in my hair, pulling me close as his mouth found mine. The kiss was fierce, desperate, a clash of fire and shadow that left me breathless.

I responded with equal fervor, my fingers digging into his shoulders as I pulled him closer. My power rose to the surface, heating my skin. For a moment, lost in the heat of his touch and the intoxicating rush of power, I forgot about corruption and consequences and all the reasons this was a terrible idea. There was only Evander, only the burning need that consumed us both.

Reality intruded. A sound in the corridor outside, voices approaching and then moving away, shattered the spell. We broke apart, both breathing heavily, staring at each other with shock and something that refused to cool.

My lips burned where he'd kissed me. Run. Stay. Burn everything to ash. My phoenix fire surged, demanding more, while every survival instinct I'd accumulated over centuries screamed warnings. I'd been here before. Not this exact moment, but this feeling. The pull toward someone I'd inevitably lose.

"Adara—" he began, hands up, hair askew, voice rough in a way that threatened to shatter my resolve.

I fled before he could say more. The taste of him lingered on my lips as I moved through the corridors, a reminder of how close I'd come to losing control. Once this was over, I'd leave. I always left.

My powers flickered beneath my skin, fire and shadow intertwining. The sensation should have terrified me. It didn't. That was the problem.

I wasn't watching where I was going, too lost in my own tumultuous thoughts. Which is why I nearly collided with Evander as he materialized out of the shadows in front of me.

"Adara, wait—" he hissed, reaching for my arm.

Before I could respond, the sound of approaching footfalls echoed down the hallway. Evander's eyes widened, and without warning, he pulled me into a small alcove hidden behind a tapestry. We were pressed close together in the tight space, his body warm from the fresh blood, solid against mine in a way I was trying very hard not to notice.

"What are you—" I started to hiss, pushing him away, but he pressed a finger to my lips, silencing me. He flicked his fingers and shadows wrapped around us, sheltering us from prying eyes.

The voices grew clearer, and I recognized Thane's imperious tone.

"The containment is failing faster than anticipated," Thane was saying. "We need to accelerate our plans."

"But sir," another voice protested, "the risks—"

"Are nothing compared to the opportunity it presents," Thane cut in. "With that kind of power at our disposal, we could reshape the very fabric of reality itself. A few... losses are an acceptable price."

My eyes met Evander's in the darkness, shock and anger mirrored in his gaze. This was worse than we'd imagined. The coven wasn't just studying the portal. They were actively planning to use it as a weapon. Or, at least Thane was.

We stood frozen, barely daring to breathe as the voices faded down the corridor. Silence fell, and the rest of my senses rushed back. The solid press of Evander's body against mine, the way his arm had tightened protectively around my waist when Thane's voice first reached us, the thundering of my own heart that had nothing to do with fear of discovery. Every point of contact burned, a stark counterpoint to the cold political calculation we'd just overheard.

"Adara," he said softly, his breath ghosting against my ear. The intimate whisper was jarring after Thane's clinical discussion of acceptable losses. Heat flashed through me. I squirmed against him before I could stop myself. "I think we may have gravely underestimated the situation."

I tried to focus on the threat rather than the way his body tensed in response to my movement.

"They're not just trying to contain it. They want to harness it. Use it. Weaponize it." I rubbed absently at my left leg where the spiral scars from the Mage's Council's containment magic twisted upward. Their methods had marked me once before. I wasn't eager to see what vampire containment magic might do. I met his eyes, searching for any hint of prior knowledge while painfully aware of how close our faces were.

"Did you know about this?"

He shook his head, looking genuinely troubled. "No. I suspected Thane had ambitions beyond simple containment, but this... this is pure madness."

We remained pressed together in the alcove, his body still warm from his recent feeding, a stark contrast to the cold stone at my back. I should have pulled away, put some distance between us. But I stayed rooted in place, drawn to the intensity in his gaze. Perhaps I feared our eavesdropping would be discovered? I wanted to tell myself that's why I stayed. The lie didn't hold.

"We need to stop them," I said, my voice barely above a whisper. "Whatever they're planning, it could tear reality apart."

Evander nodded, his expression grave. "Agreed. But we'll need proof. Something concrete to present to the council, or at least to those members who might listen to reason."

I arched an eyebrow. "And how do you suggest we get that proof? I doubt Thane's going to kindly hand over his diabolical plans if we ask nicely."

A slow, dangerous smile spread across Evander's face. "No, but I might know where he keeps his private records. Care for a bit of breaking and entering, Lady Ashwing?"

Despite everything, I smiled back. "Why, Lord Nightshade, I thought you'd never ask."

We slipped out of the alcove, our steps perfectly matched as though we'd been partners for centuries rather than days. The heat between us hadn't dissipated. It had transformed into something more dangerous: trust. As we made our way back to Evander's chambers to plan our next move, something bigger was coming. I felt it in my bones, in the way my fire stirred restlessly beneath my skin. The fate of the realms might hang in the balance, but it was the way Evander's hand brushed against mine as we walked that truly terrified me. Saving the world was one thing. Risking my heart was quite another.

CHAPTER 7

SHADOWS AND SUBTERFUGE

ADARA

WE'D GRADUATED FROM DUSTY BOOKS TO PLOTTING a heist. Evander's chambers had transformed into a war room, with scrolls and maps littering every surface. The carefully organized research of days past had given way to controlled disorder, though he still arranged his quills by size. Vampires and their compulsive need for control, even in chaos.

I sorted through another pile of papers. "Please tell me you have a section in your library titled 'Heists for the Magically Inclined.'"

"It's filed under 'Creative Acquisition Techniques,'" he replied without missing a beat. "Right between 'Dramatic Entrances' and 'Elegant Escapes.'"

"Your filing system is remarkably specific."

"We've had centuries to hone our organizational skills. Though I must say, this is the first time I've had to create a category for 'Phoenix-Assisted Breaking and Entering.'" He turned back to the map. "Thane's private quarters are here," Evander said, pointing to a faraway section of the fortress. His finger traced a path through a maze of corridors. "The guard rotations are trickiest near the western approach, but if we time it right, during the daily council meeting, then I think we have a chance."

I leaned in to study the map. His fingers brushed mine as he outlined the route. I ignored the tingle. Tried to, anyway. "And you're sure he keeps his records there? Not in some secret vault beneath the fortress?"

Evander's lips quirked, an expression that softened his aristocratic features in a way I refused to find charming. "Thane keeps his secrets close. Like trophies on display. His ego demands an audience."

We spent the next hour refining our plan, Evander sketching patrol schedules from memory while I plotted our escape routes. For races destined to be at odds, we moved around each other with an ease that was... troubling.

"Your guard rotation diagrams are impressively detailed," I observed, peering over his shoulder. "Though I notice you've marked all the suspiciously shadowy corners. Planning our getaway or picking spots for brooding?"

"A vampire must maintain certain standards," he replied with mock severity. "What's the point of a daring escape if we can't pause on occasion to pose menacingly?"

"Ah yes, the ancient art of tactical brooding. My mistake."

Working with him was almost... fun. Like fitting puzzle pieces I wasn't sure I wanted to complete. If breaking into a vampire noble's quarters to uncover potentially realm-shattering secrets could be considered a good time.

"We'll need a distraction," I mused, tracing a finger along one of the corridors. "Something to draw attention away from our approach. Perhaps something that doesn't scream 'the phoenix did it.' Though that does narrow our options considerably."

Evander's eyes gleamed with mischief, a look that did interesting things to my pulse. "I might have an idea about that. How do you feel about causing a small magical accident in the research chamber?"

"Define small, Nightshade. I'd rather not bring the entire fortress down on our heads. Phoenix magic isn't exactly subtle. It tends to leave rather obvious evidence. Though with more fire. And possibly screaming."

He chuckled, a low sound that struck flint in a part of me I'd thought fireproof. "Nothing too dramatic. Just enough chaos to keep eyes turned away from us."

As we finalized the details, my flame-script flickered a warning. We'd drawn close over the map. Too close. The warmth still lingered in Evander's body from his recent feeding, a stark contrast to the chill that perpetually clung to the fortress.

"Your penmanship is immaculate." I watched him label another section of the map. "Let me guess. Vampire finishing school? Advanced Calligraphy 101: Writing Menacingly Through the Ages?"

He shot me an amused glance. "You jest, but you should see our actual curriculum. Immortality leaves plenty of time for honing one's handwriting."

"Of course. Can't have sloppy writing in your grimoires of doom. What would the other covens think?"

"Precisely. Though I did get reprimanded in Brooding

201 for excessive eyebrow arching. Apparently there's such a thing as too mysterious."

His scent wrapped around me. Cold stone and ancient shadows, mixed with something darker, uniquely vampiric and laced with night-blooming jasmine from his latest meal. I caught myself leaning closer before I could stop. And wasn't that just typical? Even his scent was annoyingly perfect. Like everything else about him, it seemed deliberately calculated to get under my skin. I shook my head and forced myself to focus. Now was not the time for distractions, no matter how alluring.

"It's time we got going," Evander said, his voice low and intense. My flame-script flared in response. Traitor. "The next council meeting is due to start. Are you ready for this, Phoenix?"

I met his gaze, letting a slow smile spread across my face. "Oh, vampire. I was born ready. The question is, can you keep up? Or do I need to leave a trail of blood through your maze of a fortress?"

His answering grin was all fang and promise, a predatory expression that should have triggered every survival instinct I possessed. Instead, it sent heat coursing through my veins. "I suppose we'll find out, won't we?"

As we made our final preparations, my flame-script pulsed uneasily. We were about to cross a line. Whatever we discovered in Thane's quarters would change everything. For the coven, for the realms, and for us. The weight of it settled on my shoulders, a familiar burden. Somehow lighter when shared with him.

But as I glanced at Evander, his face set in lines of determination, something flickered to life in my chest.

Something I hadn't experienced in centuries: hope. Maybe, just maybe, we could actually pull this off. Though I'd never admit that his presence was part of that hope.

"Let's go make some trouble," I said, extinguishing the candles with a wave of my hand. "What's the worst that could happen? Besides painful death, eternal imprisonment, or, worst of all, having to attend another council meeting."

Shadows pooled around us as Evander's power rose. Together, we slipped out of his chambers and into the darkness beyond, ready to uncover whatever secrets lurked in the heart of the Crimson Veil. The night air wrapped around us, cold and watchful, as we approached the western wing. His mastery was impressive, his eyes gleaming faintly as his shadows cloaked us from sight.

"Guards," he whispered, his breath barely disturbing the air near my ear. His proximity made my flame-script warm beneath my skin. I steadfastly ignored it. "Two of them, just around the corner. We'll wait here until they pass."

I nodded, my own senses stretching out. The coppery tang of blood magic hung heavy in the air, a testament to the vampire wards protecting this section of the fortress. "I can feel the wards," I murmured. "They're... hungry. Searching."

Evander's lips thinned. "Thane's work, no doubt. We'll need to be careful."

"Careful is my middle name," I quipped. Evander raised an eyebrow. "What? It could be. You don't know all my names. I've had quite a few over the centuries."

"Somehow, I doubt that." His lips twitched. "Unless 'careful' is spelled 'c-h-a-o-s'."

I flashed him a grin, adrenaline surging through me. "Time for our distraction, wouldn't you say? Unless you'd prefer to stand here trading witty banter all night. Though I have to admit, your snark has improved considerably since we met."

Evander nodded, his expression growing serious even as his shadows curled playfully around my ankles. "Remember, nothing too—"

"Dramatic. Yes, yes, I know." I winked at him. "Just a little chaos to keep things interesting. Think of it as... redecorating. With fire. Besides, your fortress could use a little livening up."

Before he could protest further, I reached out with my power, finding the delicate balance of energies in the research room. With a push that may have been slightly less gentle than intended, I nudged one particular experiment off-kilter.

The resulting explosion sent vibrations through the stone floors. Shouts of alarm echoed through the corridors. Evander shot me a look that was equal parts exasperation and reluctant admiration, his shadows tightening around us protectively. A gesture I pretended not to notice.

"That's your idea of 'subtle'?" he hissed. "I said distraction, not demolition."

I shrugged, unrepentant. "It worked, didn't it? Finesse is difficult at a distance. Besides, now we know where not to store volatile alchemical components. I'd call that a public service, really."

And indeed it had worked quite effectively. The two

guards we'd spotted earlier rushed off toward the commotion, leaving our path clear. We eased past the temporarily abandoned post, Evander's shadows shielding us from any remaining watchful eyes. The way his power curled around me always made my flame-script pulse in response. Not unpleasantly. Inconvenient, that.

As we approached Thane's quarters, the air grew thick with power. The blood wards pulsed with malevolent energy, seeking out any unauthorized presence. They brushed against my skin, searching, probing. They reminded me of snakes, if snakes were made of magic and murderous intent.

"Let me handle this," Evander murmured, stepping forward. "Unless you'd like to test how these wards react to phoenix fire?"

"Tempting," I whispered back, "but I suppose we should save the major explosions for our grand finale. Show me your tricks, shadow dancer."

He raised his hands, his fingers moving in intricate patterns as he wove shadows into the very fabric of the wards. The blood magic twisted and writhed, trying to resist his manipulation. But Evander was relentless, brow furrowed in concentration as he bent the wards to his will. The display of power was... impressive. And if I found the intensity of his focus oddly attractive, well. That was my problem.

With a final, decisive gesture, the wards parted like a curtain. Evander sagged slightly. The effort had taken its toll. Without thinking, I stepped closer and let my warmth steady him.

"Show-off," I said softly, genuine admiration coloring my tone.

He straightened, a hint of his usual smirk returning. The proximity between us felt charged. Dangerous. And it had nothing to do with our opposing natures. "I aim to please."

I bet you do. I suppressed a sigh. *Down, girl.*

We slipped into Thane's quarters, the door closing silently behind us. The room was opulent, dripping with the kind of ostentatious wealth that spoke of centuries of hoarding power and influence. The decor screamed 'I'm rich enough to buy taste but chose this anyway.' I half-expected to find a vampire decorating guide on the shelf: Chapter One - Why Every Surface Should Be Either Black Marble or Blood-Red Velvet.

But beneath the trappings of luxury, an overwhelming emptiness filled the room. It made my skin crawl.

"Let's make this quick," Evander said, moving toward the massive ebony desk that dominated one corner of the room. "I don't fancy overstaying our welcome."

"What, worried we'll miss the fortress's midnight brooding session? I hear it's quite the social event." I followed him to the desk. "Though I suppose breaking and entering does put a damper on our invitation status."

"Adara," Evander drawled back, a touch of warning in his tone.

I nodded, taking the bookshelves. "Look for anything related to the portal or unusual magical artifacts. Though with Thane's ego, he'd probably label it all 'Top Secret Evil Plans' in decorative golden calligraphy."

A few minutes of searching yielded nothing on the

shelves, so I turned my attention to the desk. Meticulously, I opened each drawer and sifted through the contents, frustration mounting with each fruitless search. Just as I was about to give up, my fingers brushed against an uneven surface at the back of one drawer. Intrigued, I pressed against it, and a secret panel clicked open, revealing a hidden compartment. Inside, I found a stack of documents. Clutching the papers, I motioned for Evander. He needed to see this.

My hands trembled as we sorted through the papers. Each new document sent my inner flame guttering lower, shrinking back from what we'd found. Power readings that shouldn't be possible. Reality-warping calculations that defied natural law. We spread the documents across the desk. Patterns emerged, diagrams and numbers weaving a picture neither of us wanted to see. The corruption spread rates alone were enough to make my centuries-old magic recoil.

"Evander," I called softly, the paper crackling with barely contained energy in my grip. "I think we might have underestimated just how deep this goes. And I say that as someone who's quite used to things going catastrophically sideways."

He moved to my side, his eyes widening as he scanned the document. "By all the shadows," he breathed. "They've mapped the portal and are theorizing how it came into being. There's even an incantation here to 'knock on the door', which would align the portal to your intentions. I... I think they want to harness it and then replicate it."

The implications hit us both at the same time. If the Crimson Veil succeeded in harnessing and then creating their own portals, the balance between realms would be shattered. The potential for destruction was... unthinkable, even by my admittedly high standards for catastrophe.

"Every time they tried to lock it down, it got bigger," I said, my excitement momentarily overriding my growing unease at his intensity. "Look at these notes on the energy patterns. It was drawing power from attempts to contain it. They've basically fed it every time they tried to seal it. Like trying to stop a bleeding wound by throwing knives at it."

"Your metaphors are delightfully violent," Evander remarked, a hint of amusement breaking through his serious tone.

"Well, I could say it's like trying to cure a hangover with more wine, but that felt less on-brand for vampires," I shot back. A reluctant smile tugged at his lips.

"So, how would one properly seal such a wound?" he asked.

I glanced up, really looking at him for the first time since making the connection. His eyes were fixed on the diagrams, studying them with an attention that made my flame-script flicker uneasily. The predatory focus in his gaze was... concerning.

"You seem awfully interested in the mechanics." I took a small step back. My fire stirred beneath my skin, responding to my unease. "Almost as interested as Thane, I'd say. Should I be worried about which vampire's actually playing villain here?"

His head snapped up, genuine hurt flashing across his features before his usual mask slipped back into place. For a moment, he looked younger, more vulnerable. A reminder that beneath all the vampire nobility and carefully constructed walls, he was still just a man. "You think I'm working with him?"

"I think," I said carefully, "that power is a tempting thing. And right now, this portal could be the key to controlling a lot of it. Wouldn't be the first time someone's played nice just to get their hands on power."

For a moment, neither of us breathed. The air between us felt thin, combustible. Then something in Evander's expression cracked.

"My sister," he said softly, his voice breaking on the word. "She was the first to show signs of power loss. She's barely more than a fledgling, and watching her struggle..." His shoulders sagged, decades of careful restraint falling away. "She tries to hide it, but I see her fear when her abilities fail. The way she flinches from shadows she can no longer control. The way she pretends not to notice when other fledglings surpass her."

He ran a hand through his hair, composure finally crumbling. He looked nothing like the powerful vampire noble and everything like a brother helpless against his sister's suffering. "I don't want to control the portal, Adara. I want it destroyed before it takes anything else from us."

I studied him, the fire within me responding to the raw pain in his voice. There was something else there too. A fierce protectiveness that couldn't be faked, the kind of love that transcended even vampiric nature. Well, wasn't that inconvenient? It was much harder to maintain healthy suspicion when someone showed you their heart.

"Alright," I said finally. My inner fire surged with renewed purpose, sending sparks dancing across my fingertips as I pointed to the diagrams. "Let me tell you how we're going to wipe this thing out of existence. We can use the residual power in the artifacts to anchor a second containment circle, cutting it off from everything it feeds on. Then I can use my magic to overload the portal, draining it of power. Think of it as magical surgery, just with more potential for reality-ending disaster."

As the weight of what needed to be done settled over us, a sound from the corridor froze us both. Footsteps. Rapid. Coming closer.

CHAPTER 8

DANCING WITH DARKNESS

ADARA

TENSION CRACKLED THROUGH THE AIR AS EVANDER and I locked eyes, the sound of approaching footsteps growing louder with each passing second. Nothing like imminent death to add a little excitement to breaking and entering. We had mere moments to act before we'd be discovered in Thane's private chambers. A compromising position that would likely end with both of us facing a fate worse than death, followed by death. Though knowing vampires, they'd make sure to lecture us thoroughly about proper protocol first. I could already hear the speech: 'Before we execute you, let's review the proper channels for requesting an audience...'

He moved at vampire speed. The documents disappeared under his shirt in a blur. "Think you've got another dramatic distraction up your sleeve?" Evander whispered, his tone a mix of urgency and wry amusement. "Preferably one that doesn't level the entire wing this time?"

I flashed him a grin, despite the gravity of our

situation. "Oh, darling, I'm nothing but dramatic distractions. It's a phoenix specialty. That and rising from the ashes of particularly spectacular failures. Though I'd prefer to skip that part tonight."

With a subtle move of my wrist, I let my power seep into the air, raising the temperature in careful, controlled waves. The heat shimmer started small, distorting the space around the mounted weapons that lined Thane's walls. In the flickering candlelight, the ancient blades and ceremonial spears appeared to twist and dance. Evander's eyes turned their steel gray to molten silver as he watched my work, and something in my fire strained toward him, kindling hotter just because he was near. I winked at him, then intensified the effect.

The air rippled like water, and the weapons seemed to move of their own accord, metallic surfaces catching and bending light. Some appeared to float, others to spin slowly in their mountings. A ceremonial blade clattered to the floor with a resounding clang. The perfect alarm.

In one fluid motion, Evander wrapped us both in darkness and pulled me close, his arm steady around my waist despite the strain of maintaining our concealment. Where his power met mine, the distortion became something almost beautiful. Almost enough to make me forget we were about to be caught by vampire guards.

His breath tickled my ear as he whispered, "Ready?" A shiver ran down my spine that had nothing to do with the cold stone at my back.

I nodded, not trusting myself to speak. Proximity, danger, the thrill of our successful infiltration. It all combined into a heady rush that made my pulse race and my fire burn just beneath my skin. His shadows curled around that warmth like they belonged there, a cocoon of power that should have been impossible given our opposing natures.

Heavy footsteps thundered down the hall, racing toward the sound. As the guards burst through the door, we slipped out into the corridor. Evander's shadows clung to us like a second skin. We raced through the twisting corridors, his power providing the perfect camouflage.

Evander pulled me into a small alcove, pressing me against the cold stone wall just as a group of guards rushed past. His body shielded mine completely, his shadows creating a private world in our hidden corner. Only when their footsteps faded did he relax his grip, though he remained close, his face mere inches from mine.

"That distraction," he murmured, curiosity mixing with admiration in his voice. "How did you manage that without leaving a trace of your fire?"

I smiled. His intrigue was flattering. "Let's just say there's more to a phoenix than flames." The words came out breathier than intended, my usual swagger undermined by his closeness. "Though if you're that curious, I might be persuaded to give you a private demonstration... later."

"Clever," he breathed. The timbre of his voice affected me more than I wanted to admit. "Though I have to admit, I rather miss your usual pyrotechnics."

"Don't worry," I whispered back, despite the tension. "I'm sure I'll find plenty of opportunities to set things on fire before this is over."

I could feel the heat of his body, his familiar scent

enveloping me. Cold and dark and undeniably him. Underneath was something darker, uniquely vampiric. A reminder of what he was, what we were supposed to be to each other. Enemies. Opponents. Not... this. Not trusting each other in the dark. My breath caught in my throat.

Then, as quickly as it had begun, the moment shattered. Evander stepped back, clearing his throat, though his shadows seemed reluctant to part from me. "We should keep moving," he said, his usual smooth tone fraying at the edges. "It won't be long until they expand their search for the intruder."

I nodded, pushing away from the wall and straightening my clothes, ignoring the cold that swept through me at the loss of him. Or trying to. "Right. Back to your chambers, then? We have a lot to discuss. Like how your coven apparently decided one reality-destroying portal wasn't enough."

The journey back was tense but uneventful, Evander's power keeping us hidden from the increased patrols now combing the fortress. Every step pressed us closer in the narrow corridors, a constant reminder of how much had changed between us in so little time.

As we slipped into the relative safety of his rooms, I let out a breath I hadn't realized I'd been holding. We'd done it. But the information we'd uncovered... it changed everything. Not just for the realms, but for us. Lines had been crossed that couldn't be uncrossed.

"Well," I said, collapsing into one of Evander's plush armchairs with deliberately casual grace, "I think it's safe to say we're in deeper trouble than we initially thought.

And considering I started this evening planning light treason, that's really saying something."

Evander's jaw tightened as he produced a decanter of what I assumed was some absurdly expensive blood vintage. He poured himself a glass before offering me one, which I declined with a wave of my hand. "No thanks," I said with a smirk. "I prefer my drinks less... enriched."

"Wine, then?" he offered, and I remembered the platter of food and wine the blood servant had left earlier. I nodded, jumping up to grab an apple and a muffin which smelled of heavenly spices. Evander handed me a glass of wine, and then I curled back up in the chair and bit into the muffin.

The comfortable silence shattered as Evander finally spoke the words we'd been avoiding. "Creating their own portals," he mused, swirling the dark liquid in his glass. His shadows curled around the crystal, making the blood within shimmer like black garnets. "The ambition is staggering, even for Thane."

I swallowed a bite of muffin, the spices suddenly tasteless. "Staggering implies they might actually pull it off."

"Which may well be exactly what they're aiming for," Evander said darkly. I leaned forward, resting my elbows on my knees. He took a long sip of his drink, his brow furrowed in thought. The candlelight caught the sharp planes of his face. He was beautiful when troubled. Perhaps especially when troubled.

"The question is, what do we do with this information?"

I ran a hand through my hair. "We can't let them

succeed, that much is certain. But exposing them means admitting to our little adventure. Our only option is to destroy the portal. Then Thane can't use it to spawn others." I flashed him a grim smile. "Can you imagine the council meeting? 'Sorry I broke into your evil lair and ruined your reality-destroying plans. Moving on to the next agenda item...'"

"That is ostensibly why the council summoned you here," Evander replied, a hint of his usual dry humor returning. "I'd thought they wanted such detailed maps of its power to contain it or shut it down. More fool I."

"Could Thane be at odds with the council?" I asked, watching his reaction carefully. After tonight, I was starting to read him like a second language.

Evander's expression darkened, his fingers tightening around the crystal glass until I feared it might shatter. "It's possible," he admitted reluctantly. "The Crimson Veil has always been a hotbed of political maneuvering, but this level of deception..." He trailed off, shaking his head. His shadows writhed at his sides, reaching toward me before he pulled them back.

I watched him carefully, noting the tension in his shoulders, the way his power betrayed his careful composure. "There's more you're not telling me, isn't there?" My fire stirred restlessly beneath my skin.

He met my gaze, conflict clear in his steel-gray eyes. "Adara, you have to understand. The intricacies of vampire politics—"

"Cut the crap, Nightshade," I interrupted, my patience wearing thin even as my heart ached at his obvious struggle. "We're way past political niceties. If we're going to stop this madness, I need to know everything. We've already committed crimes together. Might as well go all in."

Evander sighed, setting down his glass. He looked tired. Not the performative weariness of vampire nobility, but genuinely, bone-deep tired. "Very well. The truth is, there's been a growing faction within the coven that believes we need to take a more aggressive stance in our dealings with other realms. Thane is their de facto champion."

"And let me guess," I said, a smile tugging at my lips despite myself. "Creating portals to invade other realms fits right into their expansionist agenda. What is it with vampires and dramatic plans for world domination?"

He nodded grimly, but the corner of his mouth twitched. "Precisely. But I never imagined they'd go this far. The risks involved in manipulating reality on this scale."

"Are enormous," I finished for him. I rose to pace the length of the room, apple in hand. "We're talking potential collapse of multiple realms, not just vampire territory. Hard to argue over power when reality itself unravels."

Evander stood, matching my restless movement. "The council must be informed. If enough of them can be swayed—"

"And how many of them are already in Thane's pocket?" I countered, spinning to face him. "For all we know, half the council could be backing this insanity. Face it, your political solution is as stable as that alchemy experiment I may have slightly over-enthusiastically adjusted."

He stopped, running a hand through his dark hair. "You're right. We can't risk it. But, Adara, if we act alone..."

I moved to stand before him, close enough to feel the familiar pull between our powers. "Then you'll be branded a traitor, hunted by both Thane's faction and probably the rest of the coven too. I know." I gave him a wry smile, my heart clenching at the thought of him in danger. "Wouldn't be the first time I've gone rogue to save a realm or two. I'm guessing you have a bit more at stake."

Evander's eyes searched mine, concern welling in their depths. "I'd be risking my existence within the coven. They could excommunicate me."

"Some things are worth the sacrifice," I said softly.

For a moment, neither of us spoke. The weight of the decision hung heavy in the air between us. Then, almost imperceptibly, Evander nodded.

"So," he said, a hint of his usual smirk returning, though his eyes remained intense, "how does one go about destroying a reality-altering portal?"

I grinned, feeling a surge of that reckless energy that had gotten me into (and out of) so many tight spots over many lifetimes. "Oh, darling. I thought you'd never ask. First things first. We're going to need some very specific magical components..."

As we settled into planning, the mood shifted. "We need to move quickly," I said. "The corruption is spreading faster than ever. If we wait too long, there won't be enough power left in the artifacts to anchor another containment circle."

"Rushing in without proper preparation would be

suicide," Evander countered, stepping into my path. "We get one chance at this, Phoenix. One chance to get it right."

"We're running out of options almost as fast as we're running out of time."

His expression softened. "Then let's make every second count. You wait centuries between lives. Surely you can manage a few more days to get this right."

I held his gaze, my fire settling into something steady and sure. He didn't look away.

Let Thane and his cronies come. We had a realm to save, and I was ready to burn the whole damn place down if that's what it took.

CHAPTER 9
THE HEIST
ADARA

THE PREDAWN AIR PRICKED MY SKIN AS WE descended into the depths of the fortress. Beside me, Evander moved with that eerie stillness unique to his kind, each step calculated and predatory. His shoulder brushed mine, and that kiss still burned on my lips. A dangerous distraction when we needed absolute focus.

"The morning guard rotation begins soon," he murmured, nostrils flaring slightly as he scented the air. "We have perhaps twenty minutes before Thane's blood-bound start their rounds."

"Plenty of time," I whispered back, though my hands trembled slightly as I pushed open the research chamber door. "Unless you're getting cold feet? Well, colder feet."

His shadows coiled tighter around us both. My fire responded instinctively, making the very air ripple.

The research chamber's protective wards pulsed as we entered, old magic recognizing our presence. Relics lined the walls in careful arrangements, each secured behind layers of blood sigils and containment spells.

Someone had been paranoid about placement. The most dangerous pieces sat as far apart as possible, like feuding relatives at opposite ends of a dinner table. Except these relatives could tear holes in reality.

I moved fast, grabbing each component we needed while Evander kept watch. My fingers tingled as I lifted the first piece: a fae crystal that sang with otherworldly resonance. The dragon scales came next, their primal heat a stark contrast to the bear claws' grounding force. Each relic responded uniquely to my touch, their magics adapting and shifting, almost curious.

A distant sound echoed. Evander's head snapped up, his eyes bleeding to crimson. "Someone's coming," he hissed, fangs partially extending. The darkness around him writhed with predatory anticipation.

Flame-script flickered at my wrists as I reached for the wolf's pelt. It slipped in my grasp, nearly sliding to the floor before a coil of dark magic caught it, suspending it mid-air. I snatched it back with a nod of thanks. Our eyes met in a moment of shared panic. I drew a sharp breath. *Focus.* I grabbed the vampire teeth next, fingers steady through sheer will.

Their combined energy prickled across my skin, raising the hair on my arms as I carefully packed them into my bag. They sang to each other like a choir of angry cats. If those cats were immortal and potentially reality-ending.

"I don't suppose any of your vampire tomes mention how to get stolen relics to play nice together?" I asked, wincing as a particularly discordant pulse rippled through the air.

"Sadly, Magical Artifact Harmony for Dummies wasn't

part of the required reading," Evander replied dryly. "Though there was an interesting chapter in So You've Stolen Something Dangerous about proper storage techniques."

"Of course there was. Did it come with a complimentary guide on how to look innocent when other supernatural races come asking questions?"

"That's more of a graduate-level course."

Each piece resonated with the others now, creating harmonies that shouldn't have been possible. The portal. It had to be amplifying everything. The texts we'd studied last night had been full of cheerful warnings about mixing different magical sources and accidentally unraveling reality. My flame-script pulsed erratically beneath my skin, responding to the fear I refused to name. *No pressure.*

Another sound echoed through the corridors, closer now. Before I could blink, Evander was beside me. Vampire speed. So unfair it should be illegal. His hands gripped my waist, and the world blurred as he gathered me against his chest.

"Hold tight," he ordered, the formal cadence of vampire nobility doing nothing to mask the tension beneath. "The guards approach."

We shot through the corridors, his shadows cloaking us in darkness. The stolen relics pulsed against us, their energy responding to our merged magic in increasingly volatile ways. Running through secret passages with a vampire noble while carrying enough contraband to start a war. Leave it to the Crimson Veil to make even their escape routes theatrical. Small objects shattered in our wake as the resonance grew stronger, and his hold tightened in response.

He took a sharp turn, and suddenly we were passing through what appeared to be a solid wall; one of the fortress's hidden passages that responded to vampire blood-rights. Everything in my bag flared as we crossed the ancient wards. Light bent strangely around us, and for a moment I saw multiple versions of us. Each reflection showed us differently. In one, Evander's shadows completely engulfed my fire; in another, our magics had merged into something entirely new, neither light nor dark. My stomach lurched with equal parts fear and exhilaration.

We emerged in Evander's chambers, both breathing heavily. Even his slower vampire lungs were working overtime.

"We need to begin the preparations," I said, stepping back. The fate of multiple realms hung in the balance, yet all I could focus on was the way his shadows still reached for me, tracing patterns in the narrowing air between us.

Evander nodded, his aristocratic features settling into familiar lines of control, though his eyes retained hints of crimson. His shadows curled around my wrist for just a moment, a touch as intimate as any kiss. "Indeed. The sooner we—"

A thunderous boom shook the fortress foundations, and the portal's corruption rolled through the air like poison through veins, leaving that telltale metallic tang on my tongue.

CHAPTER 10

THE DECISION

ADARA

"THE PORTAL," I BREATHED. I RECOGNIZED THE signature of unnatural power. Each pulse felt stronger now, more focused, like it had gained a terrible awareness. The corruption had evolved beyond mere magical contamination. It was learning. Adapting.

Evander's face drained of what little color it had. "This is different from the last expansion." His shadows coiled tighter, responding to a threat that pressed against the very fabric of reality. "The energy patterns are shifting, restructuring themselves."

Panicked shouts echoed through the corridors outside, punctuating his warning. The fortress was awakening to the growing threat, and our carefully laid plans were crumbling around us.

"We need to move quickly," I said, spreading Thane's stolen diagrams across the ornate desk. The ritual layouts were complex, layers of magical theory written in his precise hand. My eyes narrowed as I traced the flow of power through his designs.

Evander moved to join me, close enough that our arms brushed as we studied the plans. My pulse quickened at the contact. His usual smirk had been replaced by intense concentration, though I noticed how his hands shook slightly as he followed the complicated sigils. "Agreed," he said, voice tight. "But we can't rush this, Adara." His eyes met mine with a weight that pinned me in place. "I won't risk losing you to haste."

The raw honesty in his voice sent heat flaring through my chest. I arched an eyebrow, covering my reaction with humor. "Oh? And here I thought we'd just draw some pretty circles and hope for the best. Your expertise is truly invaluable." The words came out softer than intended, more fond than sarcastic.

He shot me a look that was equal parts exasperation and affection, though I caught the shadow of fear still lingering in his eyes. "Your wit never fails to amuse, Phoenix," he murmured, reaching for another diagram. "Now, shall we focus on potentially saving multiple realms from destruction?"

I sorted through the ritual diagrams, centuries of magical knowledge guiding my assessment. Thane's work was brilliant but fatally flawed. His obsession with amplification would doom his design to catastrophic failure. My fingers moved across the pages, already seeing how phoenix fire could transform what he'd intended to destroy.

"These power flows," I murmured, studying the intricate patterns. "He's trying to create a circuit, using the portal's own energy to fuel the replication. But he's missing something fundamental about the nature of power."

I sketched quick modifications on the margin of his diagrams, my phoenix instincts guiding my hand. "The key isn't in containing or amplifying. It's in transformation. Like how phoenix fire doesn't just destroy, it renews." I followed the modified patterns with my fingertip. "If we reverse these channels here and here, we could create a conversion field instead of an amplification loop. Turn the portal's energy back on itself."

Evander leaned closer, his expertise in blood magic adding another layer of insight. "The vampiric warding patterns could be adapted too," he said, pointing to a series of complex sigils. "These are meant to draw power from the coven's collective strength, but if we modify the flow..." His fingers sketched new patterns alongside my notes.

"We could use it to ground the wild energies instead," I finished, our minds working in parallel. "Though managing the power requirements for that kind of modification would take incredible precision. One mistake in the timing..."

"I'm well aware. But look here," Evander said, his voice carefully neutral as he tapped a particular layout. "The bear claws could ground the wild energies if we modify this configuration." He straightened, putting a careful distance between us, though his gaze lingered when he thought I wasn't looking.

I studied the section he'd marked, noting how the placement of the wolf's pelt could create a natural barrier against magical backlash. "The resonance will be stronger this way," I said, comparing the energy flows Thane had mapped.

"We're breaking all the old rules by working together," he mused. "Is playing the outlaw typical for you?"

I smiled, though it felt bittersweet. "Story of my lives. Though I have to admit, you've added some interesting new chapters." I paused, considering. "Most of my previous volumes didn't include quite so much brooding in shadows or perfectly tailored black clothing. The commitment of your kind to your style is truly remarkable." I ran a finger along one of his notations on the diagram, admiring the precise elegance of his modifications. "And I'm impressed. You seem to actually know what you're doing."

His lips quirked in that familiar half-smile that now held so many layers of meaning. "Your faith in me is truly touching, Adara." He stepped closer, his hand brushing mine as we both reached for the same page. My flame-script flared, traitorous as ever. "I'll cherish this moment of approval for centuries to come."

The casual reference to his immortality sent an unexpected pang through me. Before I could examine that feeling too closely, another tremor shook the room. Stronger this time, accompanied by the sound of shattering glass somewhere in the distance. The diagrams scattered across the desk, and I quickly gathered them before they could fall. A page caught my eye. One of my earlier modifications to the power flow. In my haste to appear collaborative, I'd sketched a single-channel configuration, one that would only work with a power source capable of continuous renewal. I tucked the betraying diagram beneath the others, not ready to face its implications.

Through the corridors, the portal's influence grew more tangible with each passing moment. The stones themselves recoiled from its touch, ancient wards flickering weakly against the creeping wrongness. A deep crack split the ceiling above us, raining debris as the fortress's very foundation buckled under the portal's assault. Whatever Thane had done to amplify the portal, it was working with horrifying efficiency. Typical. The one time vampires managed to be efficient about something, and it had to be about tearing reality apart.

"We're out of time," Evander said, his playful demeanor evaporating as he cast a worried glance toward the door. "The council will want answers, and they'll come looking for us soon." His darkness curled around us both, unconsciously protective. For creatures supposedly representing eternal night, vampires could be remarkably unsubtle with their affections.

Right on cue, a sharp knock echoed through the chamber. We froze, our powers instinctively reaching for each other in the moment of shared panic.

"Lord Nightshade!" The voice carried the weight of authority edged with barely contained fear. "Your presence is required in the council chambers immediately!"

Evander looked at me, his irises flashing crimson. His hands tightened on the edge of the desk, knuckles white, and his shadows pulled at me, trying to draw me closer even as duty demanded we separate.

He advanced with smooth, controlled steps to the door, easing it open just enough to address the messenger. "I'll be there shortly," he said, his voice carrying the perfect blend of aristocratic annoyance and bored compliance. "I need to secure a few items that were knocked over in the blast."

I held my breath, impressed despite myself at how smoothly he lied. But then, he'd had decades of practice navigating vampire politics. The messenger hesitated, and I could almost feel their suspicion pressing against the door. "That is... unfortunate, my lord. Make haste, as I will wait to accompany you. The situation grows more dire by the moment."

The threat in those words was subtle but clear. They didn't trust him; perhaps they already suspected something. Evander closed the door and turned back to me, and his careful mask slipped. Something raw and unguarded surfaced beneath it, something that made my phoenix fire reach for him before I could stop it.

"We need a plan," he whispered urgently, moving close enough that his breath stirred my hair. His hand found mine, fingers intertwining with an intimacy that felt both new and achingly familiar. Warmth pulsed through me, my fire recognizing his touch. "I can't avoid the council meeting without raising suspicion, but leaving you here..."

"Go," I said, surprising myself with the decisiveness in my voice, even as everything in me protested the idea of separation. "I'll continue the preparations here. We can't risk them discovering what we're planning." *Or how close we've become,* I added silently.

His eyes searched mine, conflict clear in their depths. "Adara, are you sure? If they find you here..."

"Then I'll charm them with my sparkling wit and devastating good looks," I quipped, though the humor felt hollow even to my own ears. My hand rose of its own accord to trace the line of his jaw, fire meeting ice in a caress that should have hurt us both but instead sent warmth pooling deep in my chest. "I can handle myself, Evander. You should know that by now."

For a moment, I thought he might argue. The intensity in his gaze made my breath catch, something fierce and barely leashed burning behind those crimson irises. Then, with visible effort, he straightened his posture and let his aristocratic mask slide back into place. "Very well," he said.

As he left for the council meeting, Evander paused at the door. His hand gripped the handle, metal creaking under the strain of his control.

"Be careful, Phoenix," he whispered, the words carrying weight far beyond their simple meaning.

Then he was gone, taking his shadows with him but leaving their echo branded into my power like a promise. I stood alone in his chambers, surrounded by the evidence of our conspiracy: diagrams and notes that held the potential to reshape or destroy multiple realms. And all I could think about was the empty space where he'd been standing.

I turned back to Thane's diagrams, focusing on the intricate weave of power flow, but my mind kept catching on my modifications. Each line I'd drawn held implications I wasn't ready to face, possibilities that would mean betraying the trust growing between us. My notes in the margins told their own story: ways to adapt the ritual for a single practitioner, calculations specific to phoenix fire, power requirements that would burn out any normal magic user.

Exhaustion settled into my bones, sudden and heavy.

My gaze drifted to Evander's canopy bed. The silk sheets carried his scent, frost and shadows and something uniquely Evander, with that subtle vampiric essence I'd grown to crave. Despite every instinct warning against it, I sank onto the edge.

His presence saturated everything: the carefully arranged books on the bedside table, the rich draperies, every detail that spoke of the man behind the vampire nobility. My eyelids grew heavy. Fragments of lives I'd lived surfaced unbidden.

Countless faces flickered through my memory: allies, lovers, enemies. All eventually lost to time while I endured. But Evander's face emerged through the blur, sharper than all the rest. The vulnerability when he spoke of his sister, the fierce determination in our shared purpose, the way he looked at me when he thought I didn't notice. He was risking everything to stop this threat.

Everything.

The realization jolted me awake. When had his fate become so entwined with my own that the thought of him risking his immortal life made something inside me revolt? Phoenix fire stirred, restless and protective. I sat up, shoving the silk sheets aside.

"Damn it all," I muttered, swinging my legs off the bed. Each step marked the battle between what I wanted and what had to be done. Thane's diagrams lay scattered across the desk. I couldn't ignore what I'd been doing any longer, not since the moment I first understood his plans. The portal was corruption given form, an endless cycle of destruction. But I knew something about cycles, about the thin line between destruction and rebirth. Every modification I'd suggested, every alternative configuration I'd sketched. They were adaptations, unconsciously crafted to harness a phoenix's unique relationship with power and renewal.

My eyes followed the converted energy flows, marking the precise points where phoenix fire could transform corruption into something new. The calculations were beautiful in their complexity, if you could overlook the whole *might tear reality apart* aspect.

The formulas were elegant in their brutality; a single practitioner with the ability to die and be reborn could channel power that would destroy any other magical being. I had drawn these modifications while pretending to analyze other possibilities. Somewhere deep inside, I'd known it would come to this.

I paced the length of his chambers, the perfected ritual calling to me with increasing urgency. Every circuit of the room pulled me between duty and... whatever had grown between us as naturally and impossibly as the theoretical frameworks we'd developed together. Feelings I couldn't allow myself to name, not when naming it would make what I had to do even harder.

"I can't ask him to do this," I whispered to myself, thinking of all the lives I'd lived and lost, all the sacrifices I'd made and would make again. The calculations didn't lie. My power could handle the conversion that would destroy any other practitioner. Phoenix fire didn't just burn; it transformed, renewed, recreated. My own notes had proven what I'd known from the start but hadn't wanted to face: This was a job for someone who could survive their own destruction.

When sunrise forced the vampires into their daytime torpor, I would perform the ritual alone. If I failed, my rebirth was assured. Evander had only one immortal life to lose, and I refused to be the one who took it from him. Better that he hate me for my betrayal than die trying to protect me.

CHAPTER 11

DARK DESIGNS
EVANDER

I STRODE INTO THE COUNCIL CHAMBER AND scanned the gathered vampires. The acoustics carried every subtle sound: the rustle of ancient robes, the scrape of a ring against an armrest, the almost subsonic rumble of the portal's distant presence. Pallor had crept into even the eldest members' faces. Unlike the raw, metallic tang of corruption that permeated the rest of the fortress, here it manifested as a cloying sweetness that clung to the back of my throat. The death scent of decaying power.

Two centuries of careful maneuvering, and I'd been reduced to this. Observer, not player. Tolerated, not respected. My exile had stripped away everything except my name, and even that carried the stain of failure. The council chamber that had once welcomed me now felt like foreign territory.

I forced the bitterness down. Resentment was a luxury I couldn't afford. Not when my only path back to power lounged somewhere in this fortress, probably setting something on fire.

Councilor Morana sat rigidly in her ancestral seat, clad in her traditional crimson but this time her gown was all ruffles. Her silver-streaked ebony hair was plaited, hanging over her shoulder, where she leisurely toyed with the end of her braid.

Thane's voice cut through the murmurs like a blade. "Lord Nightshade, how kind of you to grace us with your presence." The words dripped with sarcasm, but I caught the underlying tension. Thane was scared, and a scared Thane was dangerous.

"The surge disrupted several critical experiments," I stated, taking my place among the council. "Some matters require a more... delicate touch than others."

Thane's eyes narrowed. "I'm sure. Now perhaps you'd care to enlighten us on the progress of your pet project? The one involving our esteemed guest?"

My shadows coiled tighter at the dismissive way he referred to Adara. I forced them still, irritated by the involuntary reaction. She was a research subject. A political asset. Nothing more.

So why did "pet project" make my fangs lengthen?

I buried the reaction beneath layers of practiced nonchalance, the same mask I'd worn for two hundred years. "Lady Ashwing continues to study the portal's unique properties. Her insights have been... most illuminating."

The words came out smooth. Clinical. Exactly as I'd intended. Never mind that I'd nearly lost my composure over Thane's tone. That was about protecting my investment. Obviously.

"Illuminating?" Thane's voice sharpened. "Our powers

fade while you play scholar with a phoenix. Time runs out, Nightshade."

As Thane continued his complaints, the council chamber crackled with tension. Lady Isolde's perfectly manicured nails dug crescents into her armrests, while Lord Darius's emerald rings flashed as his hands tightened into fists. Behind Thane, three younger council members exchanged quick glances, their faces blank but their bodies angled slightly away from him. A subtle sign of dissent that gave me hope.

Morana's face betrayed nothing, her only movement the flicking of her fingers across the end of her braid. Then she spoke. "We abandon our ancient ways at our peril," she hissed, and her traditionalist faction drew closer together. The pragmatists under Thane exchanged worried glances. Even Lady Isolde, usually so careful to maintain neutrality, seemed to be gravitating toward Thane's supporters. The portal's corruption wasn't just destroying our powers. It was unraveling the political order that had held the Crimson Veil together for centuries.

I clenched my jaw. I thought of my sister, her once-vibrant eyes now dull as the portal drained her essence. Just a few years ago, before all this began, I'd found her in Father's library, floating books through the air while practicing her power control. "Look, brother!" she'd called out, her dark curls wild with excitement. "I can make them dance!" Now those same powers barely responded to her call, and her books lay untouched, gathering dust as the corruption kept her trapped between waking and sleeping, her strength ebbing with each passing day.

I couldn't save her. Couldn't stop the portal's drain no matter how much power I accumulated, how many political games I won. My sister's fading was my failure, the price of my ambition.

And now they wanted to do the same to Adara. Use her. Drain her. Destroy what made her burn so bright.

I caught that thought and crushed it. This wasn't about sentiment. I needed Adara's power accessible and under my control, not drained into Thane's artifacts. That was all. My sister's situation was tragic, yes, but irrelevant to the tactical problem before me.

The lie tasted bitter even in my own mind.

"I assure you, Councilor Thane, I am acutely aware of the situation," I said, my voice low and dangerous. "Lady Ashwing's power is unlike anything we've encountered. She may be our only hope of containing this threat."

Thane leaned forward, a predatory gleam in his eye. "Containing? No, Lord Nightshade. The time for containment has passed. We must harness this power, turn it to our advantage before it destroys us all."

Every muscle in my body went still. "What exactly are you proposing?"

"Tomorrow night, we will conduct a ceremony. Your Lady Ashwing will be at its center, whether she realizes it or not." Thane let that land before continuing. "The convergence of the moon's phase with the portal's energy spike will provide the perfect opportunity. We've already prepared the binding circles." He smiled, thin and satisfied. "When we channel her phoenix fire through the ancient artifacts, it will amplify our powers tenfold."

My hands tightened on the armrests. Thane spread his hands wide, oblivious to my reaction. Or perhaps savoring it.

"Imagine it, Nightshade. Enough power to not just resist the corruption, but to master it. The Crimson Veil will rise stronger than ever."

The implications sank in like venom. They meant to drain her. Use Adara as a living battery for their mad schemes, burn through her power until there was nothing left but ash.

My hands tightened on the armrests. This was a disaster. My entire strategy relied on Adara remaining powerful enough to leverage. If Thane destroyed her tomorrow night, I'd lose my only bargaining chip with the Coven. Two centuries of exile for nothing.

That was the problem. That had to be the problem.

Not the image of her fire extinguished. Not the memory of her laugh in the archives last week when I'd shaped shadows into dancing figures. Not the way she'd fallen asleep in my chambers yesterday, trusting enough to be vulnerable in a vampire's lair.

How could I protect her?

The question surfaced before I could stop it. I should be asking how to salvage my position, how to leverage this situation to my advantage. Instead, I was thinking about the warmth of her presence in my cold sanctuary. About copper curls splayed across my pillows.

When had that shift happened?

How could I stop this insanity before it was too late?

"And what if your plan backfires? What about the consequences?" I asked. My voice stayed steady through sheer will. "If the portal's corruption spreads beyond our borders, if we lose control—"

Thane waved a dismissive hand. "Acceptable losses. The weak will fall, and the strong will emerge triumphant."

The rage was building behind my ribs, a pressure that begged for release. I opened my mouth to argue further, but the council head's voice cut through the chamber.

"Enough," she said, her tone brooking no argument. "The decision has been made. Lord Nightshade, you will ensure Lady Ashwing's cooperation. Whatever it takes."

I bowed my head, a show of subservience that hid the fury in my eyes. "As you command."

My journey back to my chambers took me through the fortress's oldest corridors, where the remnants of ancient shadow magic still lingered. Out of habit, I paused at the memorial alcove. My father's shadow-wrought portrait hung there, its edges growing fainter as our bloodline's power waned.

He'd been a master of vampire politics. Ruthless when needed, charming when useful, always calculating three moves ahead. He would have known how to handle Thane's scheme. How to turn it to advantage, or at least ensure his own survival.

He certainly wouldn't have let himself care about a phoenix.

Soon, my sister's powers might fade entirely. My father's legacy, reduced to this. And I was no closer to redemption than the night they'd cast me out. The Nightshade name, once feared and respected, now synonymous with failed ambition.

Unless I could salvage this. Somehow.

The thought spurred me forward with renewed purpose. I had to find a way to protect Adara and my position. Both. There had to be a strategy that served both ends.

There had to be.

When I reached the door to my chambers, a familiar scent wafted through the air. Smoke and citrus, with an undercurrent of wildness that made my fangs lengthen before I could stop them.

I paused, hand on the door. Two hundred years of perfect control, and a phoenix's scent undid me. Pathetic.

I took a steadying breath, straightened my shoulders, and pushed the door open.

Adara lounged on my bed, her fiery curls splayed across my pillows, her presence transforming my carefully ordered sanctuary. The room's ambient darkness had shifted, laced with threads of gold that hadn't been there when I'd left. Her eyes were closed, her breathing slow and even. But I knew better. The slight tension in her jaw, the way her fingers twitched. She was half awake, and no doubt aware of my presence.

I closed the door behind me. Something primal stirred at the sight of her, all vulnerability and warmth in my cold sanctuary.

I should be thinking tactically. She was in my space. This was an opportunity. I could use this moment to bind her closer, strengthen her trust, make her dependent on my protection. That was how this worked. Manipulation required proximity, after all.

But beneath the calculation, something worse. A

longing I'd been trying to bury for weeks. The way her red hair contrasted against my dark sheets, the slight rise and fall of her chest. It stirred something in me I had no name for, spreading through my ribs like slow fire.

When had I started watching her sleep like some lovesick mortal? When had her safety become more important than my redemption?

I didn't have answers. Just the uncomfortable awareness that I was standing here, staring at her, and the strategic calculations felt like excuses.

I schooled my expression into something approaching amusement. Time to face the phoenix. And my own foolishness.

I leaned against the doorframe with forced casualness. "Enjoying yourself, Phoenix?" I drawled. "I must say, I never thought I'd see the day when you'd relax in a vampire's lair."

Adara's eyes snapped open, molten gold meeting steel gray. She sat up slowly, a languid grace in her movements that sent a shiver down my spine. "Well, you know what they say, Nightshade. Keep your friends close and your devastatingly handsome enemies closer."

I couldn't help the smirk that tugged at my lips. Even now, her wit didn't waver. "And which am I in this scenario? Friend or foe?"

She tilted her head. Her gaze considered me with an intensity that made me feel exposed. "That remains to be seen, doesn't it? You're looking a bit worse for wear. Rough go at the council?"

Everything I'd learned in the council chambers pressed against my teeth, demanding to be said. But caution held my tongue. I needed to be sure, to know where we truly stood.

"You could say that," I replied, sinking into a nearby chair. "The council is... restless. The portal's effects are becoming harder to ignore."

She swung her legs off the bed, leaning forward with an excitement that was almost contagious. "We'll close it, Evander. That should relieve some of their restlessness."

My mind raced with the danger she was placing herself in. "Adara, listen to me. Whatever you're planning, whatever you think you need to do, don't. Not yet. The council isn't trying to fix the portal. They have other plans for you."

She rose to meet me, heat blazing in her eyes. "Then tell me, Evander. No more half-truths, no more political double-speak. What the hell is really going on?"

I stared at her, caught between my duty to the coven and my growing, undeniable need to protect her.

No. Not just need. Want. I wanted her safe in a way that had nothing to do with strategy.

The realization settled like a stone in my chest.

"They're planning to use you," I said, my voice barely above a whisper. "Tomorrow night, during the ceremony. They want to turn the ritual against you and drain your power, to harness it for their own ends. And I don't think they care if you survive the process."

The words came out clinical. Detached. As if I were reporting on a political maneuver, not the potential destruction of someone who'd somehow slipped past every defense I'd built in two centuries.

Adara's eyes widened, a mix of shock and... was that

betrayal? "It wouldn't be the first time I was viewed as a tool instead of a person. And you?" she asked, her voice tight. "Where do you stand in all this?"

And there it was. The question I'd been avoiding since that first night in the archives when she'd laughed at my shadow-dragons.

I should tell her I'd help protect her interests because they aligned with mine. That I needed her power intact to regain my standing. That this was tactical, calculated, a mutually beneficial alliance.

It would even be partially true.

I moved closer, close enough that the warmth radiating from her skin cut through the chill of the chamber. Close enough to see the gold flecks in her eyes, the way her pulse beat at her throat.

"With you."

The words escaped before I could analyze their wisdom. Before I could dress them up in political language or qualify them with strategic caveats.

I waited for regret. For the cold calculation that had kept me alive through centuries of vampire politics. Instead, there was only certainty. Terrifying, unprecedented certainty.

"Shadows help me, Adara, but I'm with you."

Decades of careful political maneuvering, and here I was, pledging allegiance to a phoenix based on nothing but instinct and impossible trust. My father would be appalled. The Crimson Veil would see it as weakness.

And I couldn't bring myself to care.

That, more than anything, told me how far gone I was.

For a long moment, we stood there, the air between us

charged with tension. Then Adara nodded, a fierce determination settling over her features. "Then it's simple. We move before they're expecting it and close the portal before they have the chance to act."

Her voice gave me pause. A too-careful casualness, perhaps, or the way her eyes wouldn't quite meet mine when she said the words. "We'll need to coordinate perfectly," I said. I watched her reaction closely. "The positioning of the artifacts, the timing of the power channeling..."

"Of course," she replied smoothly. Too smoothly. "I'll need to meditate tonight, prepare my power. But tomorrow, when the sun is highest and your kind are at their weakest..." The mention of high noon sent an instinctive shudder through me. She trailed off, and I caught a flicker in her expression. Guilt? Determination? She masked it with a smile before I could decide. "Because I'll be damned if I let a bunch of power-hungry bloodsuckers use me as their personal battery."

I should have pressed her further, should have demanded complete honesty. But the warmth of her presence, the fierce set of her jaw... I nodded, grateful she believed me.

A slow smile spread across my face. Watching her plan our impossible rebellion with the same fire she brought to everything, I felt something shift in my chest.

I should examine that feeling. Categorize it. Control it.

I didn't want to.

"Damned indeed." I closed the distance between us. "You never stop surprising me, Phoenix."

I reached out. My fingers ghosted along her jawline.

The heat of her skin burned through me, sharp and undeniable. Her eyes met mine, gold burning with an intensity that matched the fire beneath her skin.

Every instinct I possessed screamed that this was dangerous. Vampires who let their hearts rule their heads rarely survived the centuries. Attachments were weaknesses to exploit. Caring was a luxury I couldn't afford, not when I was still clawing my way back from exile.

I told myself this was strategy. Bind her closer. Make her trust me. Secure my position.

But as my shadows curled around her, the justifications crumbled. This wasn't about survival or strategy or redemption. This was about the way she'd fallen asleep in my chambers. About her laugh echoing through ancient corridors. About how she made me feel less like a political creature and more like...

I didn't finish the thought. Couldn't.

She grabbed the front of my shirt and pulled me closer. Every calculation I'd ever made fell away.

Two centuries of control, destroyed by a phoenix with copper curls and terrible ideas.

I crushed my lips to hers. She tasted of fire and defiance, fierce and bright against the darkness I carried. My hands tangled in her curls as I deepened the kiss, pouring into it everything I couldn't say. Everything I was still afraid to name.

For once in my long, calculated existence, I stopped thinking three moves ahead. I stopped scheming. I just... felt.

It should have terrified me.

It did terrify me.

I kissed her anyway.

When we finally broke apart, both of us breathing heavily, I rested my forehead against hers. "No matter what happens," I promised, "I'm with you."

CHAPTER 12
THE NIGHT

ADARA

I PULLED BACK SLIGHTLY FROM EVANDER'S "I'M with you," studying the sharp aristocratic features I'd come to know so well, the careful mask of control finally cracking. The silk sheets pooled around my waist as I shifted in the ornate four-poster bed, my skin bare in the dim candlelight of his private chambers.

His fingers followed each of my exposed scars with reverent care. The burn patterns on my forearms, the spiral marks climbing my legs, the claw marks across my collarbone. Each touch was an acknowledgment of the battles I'd fought, the choices I'd made. His eyes held not pity for these marks, but understanding of what they'd cost me.

As my fingers brushed along his jaw, the charged moment stretched between us, want and restraint balanced on a knife's edge. His shadows curled around us protectively while my glow intensified, light and dark dancing together as my phoenix fire pulsed in recognition, flame-script flaring to meet him.

Well, wasn't this just perfectly poetic. A phoenix and a vampire finding harmony. Somewhere, I was certain, the Fates were either laughing themselves silly or patting themselves on the back for their matchmaking skills. Probably both.

His steel-gray eyes searched mine, hints of crimson betraying his slipping control. In their depths, I found a vulnerability I'd never seen there before, raw and aching. I threaded my fingers through his hair, exploring the angular planes of his face, pale skin cool and smooth beneath my touch. His scent enveloped me. Aged parchment and winter nights mingled with something uniquely Evander.

I studied his face, doubt creeping in despite the intensity of our connection. "Are you sure about this?" I whispered. "I've only ever brought danger to those close to me."

"That may be so," he admitted, his voice rough with emotion. "But I know what I'm risking. I'm committed to following this path through with you, whatever the cost. My sister..." He faltered, shadows writhing in agitation around us. "I've watched her fade, day by day, as this corruption spreads. Watched the light leave her eyes, her powers slip away. I can't lose anyone else."

My breath caught in my throat. The arrogant vampire nobleman, the carefully constructed walls, all of it had fallen away, leaving only the man beneath. One who had already lost so much and stood to lose even more. His pain was written in every line of his body, in the tremor of his shadows. I'd lived long enough to recognize grief that ran deeper than words could reach. "I understand," I said softly, letting my own walls drop. "In all my lives, I've watched those I care about suffer. Watched them age and die while I remained unchanged, knowing I'll rise again but they never will. It never gets easier."

His fingers drew fiery patterns on my skin. Sparks of desire danced along my nerve endings. I moaned softly as his hands explored my curves, mapping every dip and swell with reverent hunger. I arched into his touch, craving more, needing to feel him against me, within me.

"Adara," he breathed, my name rough with need. "We don't know what tomorrow will bring. If we only have this one stolen moment, let's make it count."

I couldn't agree more. I tangled my fingers in his hair and pulled him down, pouring every denied want into the crush of my mouth against his. If tonight was all the Fates would grant us, I intended to brand it upon my soul for the countless lifetimes to come.

I nipped at his bottom lip, relishing the growl that rumbled through his chest. His hands gripped my hips, pressing me flush against him, and the solid heat of his body against mine sent my thoughts scattering.

We stripped away pretense and propriety, need overwhelming all our careful restraint. I gasped as his fingers found my slick folds. He stroked. Teased. "Evander," I cried, my head falling back in ecstasy. He took advantage. His mouth dragged a slow path down my throat, fangs grazing sensitive flesh.

I reached for him. The hard evidence of his need pressed against me as our bodies aligned more closely. My hand wrapped around his length, exploring its rigid contours even as he continued his unrelenting attention to my body. With each measured stroke, his control cracked a little further, fragile ice under the heat of my touch.

I wrapped my legs around his waist and pulled him closer. He complied with a groan, the thick length of him pressing insistently against my core. "Please," I panted, nails raking down his back. "I need you."

In one swift thrust, he filled me, stretching and claiming. I cried out, pleasure and pain fused, sharp and sweet, consuming me. He stilled for a moment, allowing my body to adjust before setting a deep, deliberate rhythm that left me gasping.

Pleasure coiled tighter with each drive of his hips, each drag of his fangs along my pulse point. Our panting breaths mingled in the charged space between us, the room shrinking to nothing beyond skin and heat and want.

The barely leashed hunger showed in the tension of his muscles, in the crimson bleeding into his irises. Our bodies slid against each other, the friction delicious and maddening. The wet sounds of our joining filled the room, punctuated by the thundering of our hearts.

Our eyes met. His attention shifted to my neck, pupils dilating, and then he flinched. He started to pull back, fighting his nature, but I made the choice for us both. "It's okay," I whispered. "I trust you."

When his control finally snapped, I cried out as his fangs sank deep into my throat. The sharp pleasure-pain sent shockwaves through every nerve I had left. I welcomed the exquisite sting of his bite, reveling in the erotic pull of him drinking from me, my essence flowing into him in a dizzying rush.

My world narrowed to the slide of his body in mine and the hot, wet suction of his mouth at my throat. Our powers surged and twined, fire feeding shadow feeding fire, until I couldn't tell where I ended and he began.

Power exploded behind my eyes, fire and shadow merging until his memories bled into mine and mine into his. Evander shuddered against me, whispering something in the ancient vampire tongue. My blood sang in his veins, the essence of the phoenix flooding his system. We were one. Not vampire and firebird, but a new being entirely, forged in fire and shadow.

Release crashed over us. I clung to Evander as ecstasy swept through me, his name a broken prayer on my tongue. He answered with a hoarse shout, spilling deep inside me as ancient magics crackled over our skin.

In the aftermath, we lay entwined, hearts hammering in sync. *Very dignified, Ashwing.* Having a meltdown in the arms of an immortal vampire. At least I had the presence of mind to be horizontal.

Evander's head rested in the hollow of my throat, his tongue laving the mark he'd left. Each touch was a bittersweet reminder that this night, this union, was all we'd ever have. My vision blurred as I held him close, memorizing every sensation.

"I never thought I could have this," he murmured, breaking the comfortable silence. "Never thought I'd want it. But you... you changed everything, Adara."

I lifted my head to meet his gaze, seeing my own feelings reflected back at me. "In all my lifetimes, I've never known anything like this," I admitted. "Like you." *Great. Now I was being earnest. Next I'd be writing poetry.*

He smiled then, a true, unguarded smile that made him look younger, boyish. "I'm not sure if I should apologize or feel flattered."

"Definitely flattered." I grinned, pressing a quick kiss to his smirking mouth. Even as warmth spread through me, something tightened in my chest. Our time together was nearly over. The first hints of predawn gray were already threatening the horizon, an unavoidable reminder of the sacrifice I'd soon have to make.

Pushing those thoughts aside, I focused on the precious present. We stayed like that for a long while, trading secrets and soft caresses, the outside world and all its threats feeling distant and unimportant in the circle of each other's arms.

I etched each moment into my memory, hoarding them against the lonely eternity I knew waited on the other side of tonight.

We drifted in quiet intimacy, but our powers remained intertwined. Shadow and flame continued their dance across our skin, neither willing to separate fully from the other.

My fingers carded through his hair as he spoke, his voice soft with memories long buried.

"I was born into this life," he murmured. He leaned into my touch as if drawing strength from the contact. "My sister and I, we are the last of the Nightshade line, born to carry on a legacy that stretches back centuries. She was barely more than a fledgling when our world shattered. We were nobility even then. The Nightshade name carried weight in mortal circles too."

"What happened?" I asked. Shadows danced across his face.

"Our parents were killed in a vampire political coup between clans. I knew we'd be next." His jaw tightened. "The Crimson Veil offered protection, but at a price. My allegiance, my servitude, my eternal loyalty... it seemed a fair trade for my sister's safety."

My fingers skimmed along his shoulder. Tension corded the muscles beneath my touch. "You've been protecting her ever since."

"She's all I have left of family." His voice caught. "And now I'm watching her fade anyway."

"Tell me about her," I urged softly. "What was she like, before all this?"

A wistful smile touched his lips, his expression softening. "Wild. Brilliant. Utterly fearless. She used to sneak out to dance in thunderstorms, her laughter ringing through the rain. When she was young, she wanted to catch lightning in her bare hands." He glanced up at me, his gaze almost tender. "You remind me of her sometimes. That same bright, untamable fire."

I smiled, though my heart ached. "In one of my earliest lives, I knew a mortal girl named Lina who chased storms. She was a lot like your sister, fearless, full of joy and wild energy. I used to watch her dance in the rain, marveling at her spirit. She burned so brightly." I paused, lost in the memory. "She taught me that humanity isn't about how long you live, but how fiercely you love, how fully you embrace each moment."

Evander's eyes held mine, understanding passing

between us. No words needed. Just two immortals bonding over their mutual inability to keep people alive. His thumb swept along my jaw, igniting sparks beneath my skin. "Tell me more about your lives, Adara. I want to know everything."

Wrapped in shadows and flame, I told him stories. Lifetimes of love and loss, the joys and sorrows that had shaped my eternal soul.

"How do you bear it?" he asked, his voice cracking slightly. "Watching them all fade while you go on?"

The raw pain in his eyes reached into my chest and squeezed. My own grief rose to mingle with his. "I don't, really," I admitted as I let my own walls crumble. "Each life, each loss... they become part of me." I closed my eyes, memories washing over me. "They're all still here, all those lives, those loves. The pain never really goes away, but it changes you, shapes you."

His hand found mine, shadow wrapping gently around flame. "And this life? What will you remember of it?"

I looked down at him, my heart heavy with the choice I had made. "You," I whispered. "And hopefully how to close those pesky rifts, should I ever encounter them again."

In these precious final hours before dawn, we lay tangled together, watching the play of shadows and firelight on the walls. Evander told me stories of his childhood, of the mischief he and his sister used to get into. I laughed softly, trying to picture him as a carefree young boy, not yet burdened by the weight of leadership and loss.

"I wish..." he started, then trailed off, shaking his head.

"It doesn't matter. Just... promise me you'll be careful, Adara. I can't lose you too."

"I'll do my best," I whispered, knowing it was all I could offer.

He pressed a kiss to my temple, his arm tightening around me. Slowly, his breathing deepened and evened out as he succumbed to a vulnerability I never thought I'd witness in a vampire. He drifted to sleep, centuries of rigid control melting away like frost in sunlight.

His shadows remained active even in slumber, curled protectively around us both in lazy spirals. My inner fire pulsed in response.

As I watched him sleep, my flame-script constricted, a sharp ache spreading through my chest. Unwilling to waste a single second, I let my fingers map every detail of his face, burning them into memory like photographs made of touch.

His features were softer in sleep, the aristocratic sweep of his cheekbones gentled by the fading candlelight. His mouth, so often set in stern lines of authority, had relaxed into something young and unguarded. Even in unconsciousness, his shadows reached for me, creating delicate patterns of light and dark across our skin.

Each detail I memorized was both gift and wound: the slight flutter of his eyelashes against pale cheeks, the way his hair curled slightly at his temples, the barely perceptible rise and fall of his chest. As a phoenix, I recognized the bittersweet beauty of moments before ending; our kind are creatures of cycles, after all. But never had an ending felt quite so much like betrayal. *Lucky me. A thousand lifetimes and I finally found someone worth staying for, right when staying wasn't an option.*

The weight of dawn and duty settled on my shoulders. Even this deep underground, my phoenix nature sensed the approaching sunrise, an unwelcome reminder that time was slipping away.

Beside me, Evander slumbered on, oblivious, his peaceful trust a sharper pain than any I'd known in all my lives. In sleep, his hand had drifted to my knee. The innocent contact only strengthened my resolve even as it made the leaving harder.

"I'm sorry," I whispered, the words half prayer, half plea. "But this is the only way I can protect you. Some flames are meant to burn alone." The words tasted like ash. *Real inspiring, Ashwing. Very heroic.*

I bent to brush a kiss against his temple, memorizing the feel of his cool skin beneath my lips, savoring our last shared moment.

Centuries of rebirths had taught me how to move silently. I untangled my limbs from his and eased his arm from my leg. Each inch of separation felt like tearing open a wound, his shadows clinging to me, reluctant to let go.

I gathered the bag full of ritual components with trembling hands, each item inside thrumming with potential as if they knew their purpose approached.

I allowed myself one last look. He lay sprawled across the bed, hair mussed and expression unguarded, his usual imposing composure transformed by sleep into something achingly vulnerable, almost innocent.

The urge to return to the warmth of his arms and let the world fall away was overwhelming. For a heartbeat, I let myself imagine a different path, one where we faced the portal together, where I didn't have to choose between love and duty, where trust conquered the prejudices of centuries.

But even as I sank into that beautiful dream, the portal's corruption pulsed at the edge of my awareness, a rotting wound in reality that grew more insistent with each passing moment. Its sickly energy probed at my defenses, seeking any weakness, any crack it could exploit.

Everything in me wanted to crawl back into bed beside Evander, to burrow into his arms and let his shadows shelter me from the coming storm. But the only way to protect him, to protect everyone I cared for, was to face this threat alone.

With shaking hands, I set the note on the pillow beside him. I'd written and rewritten it a dozen times, trying to find the right words to explain, to apologize, to express the depth of my feelings. In the end, I'd settled for a few short lines, knowing no words could carry what I actually meant:

Forgive me.

Some sacrifices are meant for those who can rise from their ashes.

-A

I drew one last shuddering breath and slipped out into the fortress corridors, Evander's scent still clinging to my skin.

CHAPTER 13

THE RITUAL

ADARA

THE FORTRESS CORRIDORS WERE EERILY SILENT AS I made my way through them, each step taking me further from the warmth of Evander's bed. The items in my bag vibrated with energy, a stark counterpoint to the hollow ache in my chest. For items about to help me commit spectacular magical suicide, they seemed oddly enthusiastic. Then again, maybe they just appreciated the irony of a phoenix planning her own funeral pyre.

Behind me, the note lay on his pillow. Three lines that could never fully capture what I needed to say. Three lines that might be the last words he'd ever have from me.

My fingers traced my lips absently, still feeling the ghost of his kiss. "I'm with you," he'd said. My silent agreement sat like bitter ash on my tongue. But watching him sleep, seeing that rare vulnerability... it had only made this harder. In all my lives, through centuries of deaths and rebirths, I'd never found it quite this hard to do what needed to be done.

And yet I knew with absolute certainty that this was

the only way. I traced the familiar patterns of my scars, the burn marks and spirals and silvery claw marks that mapped every magical catastrophe I'd survived. Each one proof that I could endure what would destroy others. Even if the portal's magic consumed me, I would rise again. Evander only had one life to lose, and I refused to let him risk it.

In the pre-dawn hours, the usual bustle of vampire activity had given way to an unsettling silence, broken only by the occasional ominous rumble of the expanding portal. My footsteps echoed off the stone walls. As I neared the entrance to the ravine where the tear pulsed with malevolent force, I paused. The air here was thick with corruption, carrying the metallic tang of blood and ozone. My skin crawled, every instinct screaming at me to turn back, to return to the safety of Evander's shadows.

But I couldn't. Not when the alternative meant watching him risk everything, knowing I could have prevented it. The rift was growing stronger by the moment. Some sacrifices were worth making, even if they shattered your heart in the process.

The ravine was barely recognizable from when Evander and I had first viewed the portal together. Dead vegetation twisted into unnatural shapes, withered forms reaching skyward like supplicant hands. What had been merely corrupted ground now pulsed with veins of gray-green, spreading outward from the epicenter. The wrongness latched onto my phoenix nature, corruption seeping into the very essence of my rebirth cycle. My internal flame flickered and surged in response, fighting against the pull. And there, at the heart of it all, the tear in reality gaped like a wound that refused to heal.

I swallowed hard, steeling myself for what was to come. The ritual components grew warm against my side, eager to fulfill their purpose. With trembling hands, I began to lay out the circle, each placement precise and deliberate. As I worked, my scars responded to the gathered power. The spiral marks on my legs tingled with recognition of the containment magic. The burn patterns on my forearms shimmered in response to the fae crystals' song. Even the silvery claw marks across my collarbone pulsed with awareness as I positioned the bear claws, old magic recognizing its kin. My body remembered these magics, carried their marks. Now they would serve as both warning and guide.

The fae crystals felt lighter now, as if they'd lost mass to the surrounding corruption. As I set them at the cardinal points, their otherworldly light pushed back the creeping darkness, though dimmer than before. The dragon scales formed an inner ring, their primal force a counterpoint to the rift's chaotic pull. The bear claws and wolf's pelt I'd already woven together, creating a grounding anchor for the wild magics I was about to unleash.

The tainted air thickened as I worked. The tear understood my intentions. Each wave of force made my teeth ache and my vision swim. But I pressed on, driven by the knowledge that I was the only one who could do this. The only one who could afford to fail. At least Evander had all of our research notes and access to the remaining ritual components. If I failed, he'd have everything he needed to try again.

Finally, I placed the vampire teeth at the circle's heart, their wicked points gleaming in the sickly light. With the circle complete, I took a moment to center myself. But something prickled across my skin. The artifacts pulsed with discordant vibrations, their magics clashing instead of harmonizing. My phoenix fire recoiled from the ritual circle, as if sensing danger I didn't yet understand.

I raised the stolen staff, fingers trembling around wood that had never been mine to wield. The scroll felt lighter than it should, its supposedly powerful words suddenly as substantial as smoke. "I am Adara Ashwing," I intoned, my voice carrying the weight of countless lifetimes.

"By the eternal flame that burns between worlds, I call upon the power of—" I faltered as the ancient script writhed on the page. "Through the cycle of death and rebirth, grant me the strength to... no, that's not right." The words blurred and shifted before my eyes, familiar phrases suddenly alien.

The realization crept through me like ice. The more I tried to focus on the text, the more it twisted away from my understanding. Had the scroll been corrupted by the rift's influence? The symbols pulsed with a purple-green oily sheen that made my eyes water. Or worse, had Thane deliberately altered these words, knowing someone would attempt this ritual? Even now, I could sense the dissonance of the text infiltrating the air around me, disrupting the precise magical geometry I'd crafted.

The artifacts resonated with violent force, their competing magics turning volatile. The fae crystals shattered first, their fragments dissolving into mist. Dragon scales cracked and burst into green flames. The vampire teeth simply turned to dust, leaving behind nothing but shadows. My carefully constructed ritual circle collapsed as reality buckled around me, the corruption surging stronger, feeding on the chaos of failed magic.

I'd made it worse. So much worse.

But as I watched my plans crumble, understanding cut through the panic with sudden clarity. Phoenix fire wasn't meant for elaborate rituals or borrowed power. We were creatures of renewal, of burning away the old to make way for the new. I didn't need artifacts or ancient words.

I just needed to burn.

Abandoning the ruined circle, I stepped directly into the rift's influence. My fire rose to meet the corruption, pure and primal. Each surge cauterized the edges of reality's wound, but I was burning out with every pulse. I couldn't close it completely; I'd be consumed long before that. But I could transform it. Stabilize it enough to give them a chance.

Reality warped and twisted around me as light and darkness clashed. The air crackled with competing forces, tasting of metal and starlight.

I fed everything into the flames. The phoenix fire within me answered, searing through my blood until I felt I might burst from containing it.

As the forces built to a crescendo, I caught a flicker of movement at the edge of my vision. A silhouette I'd know anywhere, backlit by the pulsing rift. Even through the maelstrom, my body reacted to his presence. My flame-script flared, heart racing, skin warming with the memory of his touch. The passion we'd shared flashed through my mind, along with all the moments of growing trust and connection we'd built.

My concentration wavered, the forces fluctuating dangerously. I wanted to stop. To explain. To run to him. But I couldn't. Not now. Not when we were so close to ending this.

Our eyes met across the maelstrom. Everything I couldn't say passed between us in that single look.

Then the rift fought back. Its pull wasn't diminishing. It was growing, feeding off my fire instead of being contained by it. My phoenix flame guttered, and I staggered, the crushing weight driving me to my knees. I was failing. Not just failing the ritual but failing him. Evander would be left to face this alone, to watch his people fade, his sister weaken, his world crumble. The thought hurt more than the rift's crushing force.

My phoenix fire flared one last time, a desperate surge drawn from somewhere deeper than magic. And then something shifted. The sickly purple-green haze began to change, taking on hints of gold and crimson where my flames made contact. Like fire consuming tainted wood, the corruption transformed. The new pulse felt different. Not benign, exactly, but no longer actively malevolent. Instead of drawing from its surroundings, it beat with a rhythm that matched my own heart. I couldn't close the wound, but I was changing it, shifting its fundamental nature into something else entirely.

Cold touched my skin. Vampire tears. Evander had reached me somehow, his arms pulling me against him even as my body began to lose its hold on solid form. Through dimming vision, I watched tendrils of gold and crimson weave through the rift, slowing its expansion, rewriting its nature. Not a victory, perhaps, but not a complete failure either. A chance, at least, for those I was leaving behind.

I tried to tell him what I was seeing, that there might still be hope. But the words dissolved into ash on my tongue, and for the first time in all my lives, I wasn't certain I would rise again.

"ADARA!"

His voice broke through the roaring silence, raw with desperation and something that might have been love. I felt his arms tighten around me as my physical form scattered into embers. My essence drained into the transformed rift, gold and crimson dancing together like the last light of a dying sun.

I'd given them time. Given him time. Sometimes, that was the greatest gift a phoenix could offer.

CHAPTER 14
THE CURSE
EVANDER

You dare leave me with ash?

I curse you, phoenix.

Flee across lifetimes. Hide in whatever form you take.

It changes nothing.

By blood and shadow, by the eternity that chains me, I bind you to your purpose.

You cannot escape what you are or the inevitability of your rebirth.

You will rise. The darkness fed on your flames. The blight that now consumes this world awaits your flame to purge it.

And when that day comes, when the world screams for the power only you can wield, I will find you.

Because you are mine to claim. Because I have nothing but time. Because you do not get to abandon what we started.

Run, Adara.

I will be waiting.

Thank you so much for reading Ashes Before the Storm!
The next book in the series, Ashes of Destiny and Desire,
is available now.

A HUMBLE REQUEST

If you loved the book and have a minute to spare, I would really appreciate a short review on the page or site where you bought the book. Your help in spreading the word is greatly appreciated. Reviews from readers like you make a huge difference to helping new readers find similar stories.

Thank you so much for reading and supporting my work!

Candice

P.S. If you'd like to know when my next book comes out and want to receive occasional updates from me, then you can sign up for my newsletter at candicebundy.com. I promise I will never sell your email to the daemonic marketing hordes.

JOIN CANDICE BUNDY'S NEWSLETTER

Dying to dive into my next tale before the masses? Satiate your literary cravings by joining my exclusive newsletter tribe at candicebundy.com or simply tap the link below. And, because I adore my newsletter family, you'll unlock secret freebies, tantalizing tidbits, and be among the first to feast upon fresh chapters.

Sign up for my newsletter here:
https://geni.us/bundy_freebook

ALSO BY CANDICE BUNDY

Adara Ashwing Adventures

Ashes Before the Storm, A prequel novella

Ashes of Destiny and Desire

Tempest of Passion and Power (2026)

The Stolen Legacy Series

Looted Legacies, A prequel novella

Forbidden Fates

Entangled Essence

Hidden Hearts

Reckless Rapture

Sworn Spirits

Devoted Desires

Caught Between Worlds Series

Wards and Whispers, A prequel novella

Smoke and Daemons

Wine and Gods

Fire and Fae (2026)

(Smoke and Daemons was previously published

as The Daemon Whisperer)

The Shadow Series

Shadow in the City, A prequel novella

Twinned Shadow

Poisoned Shadow

Shadow Underground

Magical Midlife Mixers Series

Hocus Pocus and Pinot Noir

(set in the Shadow Series universe)

<u>Other Works</u>

Ripples, a novella

Open Rack, a contemporary short

WRITING AS CR BUNDY

The Depths of Memory Series

The Dream Sifter

Dreams Manifest

For a list of my full catalog of available titles, visit my
<u>candicebundy.com</u>/<u>books</u> page.

ALSO BY PIPER FOX

Adara Ashwing Adventures: Paranormal Reverse Harem

Academy for Reapers: Paranormal Romance

Big Wolf on Campus Series: Wolf Shifter Football Romances

The Stolen Legacy Series: Paranormal Reverse Harem

Midnight Huntress Series: Paranormal Reverse Harem

Alien Warriors of New Dilaria Series: Sci-Fi Reverse Harem

The Ironhaven Pack Series: Wolf Shifter Romances

<u>The Dragon Space Order Bride Series</u>: Sci-Fi Romance

<u>Bears of Crooked Creek</u>: A Bear Shifter Romance Series

<u>Seven Brides For Seven Demons</u>: A Demon Romance Series

<u>Last Warriors of Dilaria</u>: A Sci-Fi Romance Series

The Immortal Blood Series: Vampire Romance

About Candice Bundy

I'm Candice, a rock-climbing, coffee-powered word nerd living in sunny Denver with my partner and four feline supervisors (they let us pay the mortgage). I write spicy paranormal romance, angsty fantasy, and the occasional sci-fi romp, usually starring sharp-tongued heroines who leap before they look and heroes quick enough to catch them.

When I'm not plotting chaos, you'll find me elbow-deep in the garden, perfecting a new jam recipe, or dangling from a wall at the local climbing gym. I geek out over archaeology, mythology, and any excuse to turn big ideas into habit-hacked, real-life upgrades.

Want first dibs on new releases, cat shenanigans, and other mischief? Tap into my newsletter here or say hi online. I love hearing from fellow book dragons.

For more information:
candicebundy.com
candice@candicebundy.com

ABOUT PIPER FOX

Piper Fox writes steamy paranormal romances for sassy, strong-willed women and the sexy, alpha men who love them.

Follow her on:
Facebook: facebook.com/PiperFoxAuthor
Bookbub: https://www.bookbub.com/profile/piper-fox

www.ingramcontent.com/pod-product-compliance
Lightning Source LLC
Chambersburg PA
CBHW021713190726
48289CB00008B/2515